For nearly four years, Grady LeBrun worked in a jail as a Corrections Officer. During this time, he had the opportunity to take several courses about mental health, criminology and psychology. While working in corrections, he also had the opportunity, as part of his everyday job, to converse with people suffering from various mental illnesses. This gave him a glimpse into the lives and minds of those suffering, and he tries to accurately illustrate these illnesses in the minds of his characters.

To my wonderful friends, the only ones strong or crazy enough to put up with me on a daily basis.

And to my old co-workers, who had no choice in the matter.

Thank you all for your encouraging words and helpful criticisms.

Grady LeBrun

COCONUT COOKIES

AUSTIN MACAULEY PUBLISHERS™

LONDON • CAMBRIDGE • NEW YORK • SHARJAH

Ordering Information
Quantity sales: Special discounts are available on quantity purchases by corporations, associations, and others. For details, contact the publisher at the address below.

Publisher's Cataloging-in-Publication data
LeBrun, Grady
Coconut Cookies

ISBN 9781643788791 (Paperback)
ISBN 9781645362227 (Hardback)
ISBN 9781647503888 (ePub e-book)

Library of Congress Control Number: 2021925871

www.austinmacauley.com/us

First Published 2022
Austin Macauley Publishers LLC
40 Wall Street, 33rd Floor, Suite 3302
New York, NY 10005
USA

mail-usa@austinmacauley.com
+1 (646) 5125767

Huge thanks to Austin Macauley Publishers, who were willing to give me a shot.

– ✦ – Chapter 1 – ✦ –

"Eddie!" he heard his older sister, Cynthia, shout. "Get back here right now!"

Eddie ignored the call, choosing instead to run further into the damp morning forest, his sister's puppy, Tomo, following gleefully at his heels. He could hear Cynthia's irate pursuit growing distant.

Cynthia was tall for an 11-year-old and more than a little plump. Keeping up with her spirited six-year-old brother was already an unachievable goal; a goal made worse by the terrain, he seemed to effortlessly negotiate his diminutive form through. He weaved between trees, under branches, and over rocks and fallen logs, while Cynthia's clumsy gait left her bulling through obstacles more often than avoiding them.

Cynthia decided she'd have to wallop him when she caught up. She couldn't let Eddie get away with disobedience; it might become a habit again. She'd trained him to be submissive and dutiful, giving him a good beating whenever he didn't listen. "I'm older, so you have to do what I say," she often preached. This wasn't the first time Eddie ran off in the woods; in the past, he did so every time. It took more effort to break him of that habit than any other.

Eventually, she managed to break him, though she never doubted she could; it was just a matter of when. But now he'd run off again; the defiant little brat seemed to find some measure of his old self once Tomo came into the picture.

I never should have pestered Mom and Dad into buying me that stupid mutt! she thought. *He's too stupid to realize who his real master is, even after I wallop him. What good is a stupid dog like that?!* It was too late now though, she was stuck with them. She'd just have to redouble her efforts into training the dumb dog and in retraining her stupid kid brother. She'll definitely need to give him a good trouncing for this. Cynthia stopped to catch her breath; she could barely see Eddie anymore. No, she decided, she'll have to give him two, one for disobeying her orders and one for leaving her behind.

I don't need to catch him; I just need to outsmart him. She continued forward at a leisurely pace, deciding it was best to conserve her energy and avoid any unnecessary cardio, so she could use it properly wallop him later. Besides, she didn't know how big her brother would grow, and if he ended up taking after their father, he could end up even bigger than her! If that happened, he might try to fight back, and she couldn't have that. She had to make sure she always outweighed him and running around the forest on a wild goose chase may cost her a few pounds over time. Confident, and beaming with pride at her brilliant foresight and planning, she continued to the creek where she knew she'd find him.

Cynthia stopped when she noticed Tomo's blue leash and collar on the ground. *Three wallops,* she decided. *The stupid mutt needs to stay on its leash.*

***

Usually, Eddie wouldn't so readily ignore his short-fused sister, but on that particular day, the forest had too much majesty to offer. He ran until he could no longer hear his sister, then farther still, absorbing the natural beauty around him as it fleeted in and out of his line of sight. He always had boundless energy, running without ever-growing more than a little tired. He knew one day he'd be a track star. Nobody in school ever came close to running as fast, or for as long, as Eddie.

Eddie stopped to examine his surroundings. The trees around him weren't clustered together enough to block his vision, but he was deep enough in the forest that anything beyond the trees would be too far away to see anyway. Eddie wasn't lost though, he'd come through these woods a million times and felt confident enough to keep moving forward at a swift pace.

He turned to start off again but stopped to check on Tomo. The poodle terrier mix stared up at Eddie, panting rapidly with his tongue dangling out, but, despite that, his deep brown eyes sparkled with unbridled energy. After pausing just long enough to pick the briars and twigs out of his buddy's white streaked brown fur, Eddie and Tomo were off once more.

Fifteen minutes passed before Eddie slowed to a jog, and ten more passed before he decided to stop. Tomo didn't mind the break and used the opportunity to sit down against a nearby cypress. Initially, Tomo could only keep up with Eddie for brief periods, but over the past couple of months, Tomo's endurance had grown. "Soon you'll be out-pacing me," Eddie told Tomo with a smile. "Then I'll finally have some competition!"

Tomo wagged his tail and barked once, as if to say, "Challenge accepted."

Their parents had bought Tomo for Cynthia, but the playful puppy preferred to spend his time with Eddie, much to Cynthia's disdain. Eddie appreciated the companionship, as his sister was cold and eccentric; quick to scold and slow to praise. She was the perfect little angel when adults were around, but when left unobserved and to her own designs, she revealed a crueler side. She made Eddie do her chores, fetch her food, give her his dessert, and sometimes she even took his allowance to buy herself candy. When he fought back, she'd pinch him or squeeze his arms until they hurt. Eddie tried telling their parents once, but she put on her angel mask and feigned ignorance, even going so far as to turn it around and paint him as the bad guy. She squeezed his arms so tight that day she left bruises. In the end, she always got what she wanted, and eventually, Eddie stopped fighting back. It was easier that way.

Cynthia also found sport in mistreating Tomo, startling him with loud noises while he slept, and holding treats in front of his nose only to deny him them after a few minutes of teasing. But since Tomo was a dog and couldn't be made to do chores and had no allowance to steal, most of Cynthia's boredom was directed at Eddie. While he hated how his sister treated Tomo, it was that very treatment that caused Tomo to bond with him instead of her, so Eddie figured it all worked out well in the end. Their relationship wasn't that of master and pet, but of two friends; a couple of peas in a pod – or maybe two thralls under the same malevolent taskmaster.

Eddie reached into his pocket and extracted a small plastic bag of animal crackers. At the faint rustle of plastic, Tomo's head popped up, his wagging tail increased its tempo, rustling the parched brown leaves that had accumulated at the base of the cypress from a nearby oak. Eddie tossed a cracker, which Tomo deftly caught in his mouth midair. Eddie threw one into the air above his own head and likewise caught it in his mouth. He tossed a second cracker higher and caught it. He threw the third one higher still, but it bounced off a low hanging branch and flew off course, missing his mouth entirely. Eddie sighed at his failure, but Tomo was more than happy for it and promptly rushed over to devour the cracker. Eddie chuckled at the voracious puppy and gave him a quick rub on the head before taking off again, Tomo trailing closely behind him.

A short while later they came to a small brook no more than a couple of feet across. The creek trickled through a ravine about as deep as Eddie was tall and twice as wide, smooth, black stones lined the bed, and a few fallen logs provided footing to cross the creek further upstream, where the ravine widened to nearly ten feet across. Eddie paid the logs no heed, wanting to get into the crevice rather than cross over it. Large roots from nearby trees protruded from the dirt wall that edged the creek. Eddie used them as hand and footholds and scrambled down to perch on a large rock resting at the bottom. Tomo waited patiently at the top as Eddie double-checked his footing. Once Eddie was confident his feet were secure, he beckoned Tomo to jump into his arms. Without hesitation, Tomo leaped off the miniature cliff, fully trusting his friend to catch him. Eddie caught the puppy and placed him in a shallow area of water no more than three inches deep. Tomo wasted no time and began lapping up water as soon as his paws touched the cool liquid. Eddie likewise drank from the stream, but cupped the water in his hands rather than pressing his face into it.

Once the duo quenched their thirst, Eddie picked Tomo up and placed him on his shoulder while he climbed out the opposite side of the creek, using more out-thrust tree roots to aid his ascent. When his shoulder came to ground level, Tomo jumped off and sprinted into the woods. Eddie wasn't concerned; Tomo never ran far. Likely by the time he finished climbing, Tomo would be right back at his side, ready for the next leg of their adventure. Eddie paused when he made it back above ground level. Tomo was nowhere to be seen.

"Tomo!" he called, expecting the over-enthusiastic little puppy to come running back. To his surprise, Tomo didn't. "Tomo!" As he shouted louder, thick tendrils of worry crept their way into his chest. When again no response came, Eddie nearly panicked. "Tomo! Come here, boy!" he screamed, fearing the worst. "Tomo! Where are you!?" and with that, he sprinted away, terrified some ill had befallen his best friend.

Eddie dashed in looping circles, afraid he might miss Tomo if he traveled in straight lines, all the while calling out to Tomo. He darted through the trees until he ran out of breath, but still, he didn't stop, refusing to rest while Tomo was missing. Eventually, despite his spirit's incessant tenacity, Eddie's body couldn't keep going. He had already run several miles today, and now he wasn't just running, but all-out sprinting. Within half a minute, Eddie's oxygen-deprived brain and muscles began to falter. Unable to draw breath, Eddie's vision dimmed and distorted. Moments later, Eddie lost his sense of balance, and his legs buckled under him, the rest of his body quickly following suit.

Unable to move or breathe, Eddie choked out a few stifled sobs. Tears streamed down his scarlet cheeks, and he found himself unable to release the agonizing wail that accompanied them; instead, he choked on it. His vision twisted in cruel circles, taunting his impotence. He rolled onto his stomach, trying to get back on his feet to resume his fruitless search, but the controls to his body remained unresponsive. Mucus surged out his nostrils, further impeding his attempts to breathe. He tried to liberate the terrible wail once more but discharged the contents of his stomach instead.

So disoriented was Eddie, he didn't notice the footsteps approaching until they were but a few feet away. He looked up, and his heart lifted with what he saw. Tomo! The puppy was struggling in his sister's arms as she wrangled the collar back over his head. Other than the discomfort of the vibrant choker, he appeared perfectly fine.

Eddie closed his eyes in relief, his heartbeat began to slow as he relaxed, and he was soon capable of taking a few strained breaths. All the air he took in was abruptly, and roughly, expelled from his lungs as his sister's boot-clad foot collided with his torso. His chest lurched, and his body instinctively curled into a fetal position. The pain from the vicious kick was intolerable by itself but coupled with the forced expulsion of what little air he had, nearly rendered him unconscious. Despite his body's unwillingness to move, he found himself dry heaving, desperately trying – and utterly failing – to fill his lungs.

"Don't you ever take off and leave me behind again!" Cynthia shouted at him, but Eddie was in too much physical distress to hear her. His vision clouded once more, black spots danced across his vision. Eddie thought he was going to die. When was the last time he had a full breath of air? He couldn't remember. All he could remember was a void in his chest and the inability to fill it with air as his body so demanded. Eddie steeled his will and forced himself to inhale as deeply as he could, pain shot through his chest with the effort. He managed only a small breath, but, despite the pain, it felt like the most glorious thing his lungs had ever experienced. He took a second breath and a third. Sweet, sweet relief. He could make it; it was almost over. He went to take in another breath, but a second kick connected and unloaded everything in his stomach that hadn't already evacuated.

The immediate inhale he tried after the kick proved to be foul, as he took a portion of bile into his lungs. He hacked and gagged the best he could, but his body's normal functions hadn't recovered enough to clear the bile from his throat and lungs.

"And that's for disobeying me when I told you to come back!" Cynthia shouted before letting out a pained yelp and shouting once more. Though his lungs and stomach were in worse condition than before, his hearing had returned somewhat. Using ridiculous amounts of willpower for a task that normally required little to none, Eddie managed to turn his head enough to the side to discern what was happening.

Cynthia was frantically swinging her hand back and forth; trickles of blood flew from her fingers. In her other arm, a growling Tomo was attempting to bite Cynthia and wriggle free. Cynthia shouted words that Eddie only recognized due to the frequent arguments their parents had recently begun having. Tomo squirmed enough in her grasp to bite her other hand. Cynthia squealed once more before haphazardly tossing Tomo into the air. In Eddie's frantic search, he hadn't realized he had collapsed just a few feet from the ravine. His heart skipped a beat as he watched Tomo come perilously close to flying over the edge.

Tomo hit the ground on his side and yelped as he landed. He recovered quickly and rolled back to his feet, charging toward Cynthia. Cynthia, apparently paying Tomo no more heed after the toss, kicked Eddie again, this time in the shoulder as he attempted to crawl forward on his belly. "And that's for taking the leash off that damn mutt!" she raged. The kick forced his torso backward, and he ended up on his back again. He heard Tomo's growls and Cynthia's enraged shouts.

It took him several seconds to roll back onto his belly and witness what was happening. When he finally did, he saw Tomo viciously biting the back of Cynthia's ankle and her awkwardly kicking at him with the other foot. Because of the angle, none of the kicks landed well, and Tomo held on, trying to protect his best friend. Eddie still had trouble breathing, only able to take in shallow breaths. He tried to cry out, to put a stop to the violence, but once again, his voice failed him. Desperate to make peace, he began dragging himself forward on the ground.

Tomo's lost his grip on Cynthia's ankle, and he attempted to bite at the other one, but Cynthia proved quicker, pulling her foot back and landing a heavy kick into Tomo's side. The small dog shrieked in pain as it was sent airborne once more, this time clearing the edge of the ravine. Eddie heard a thump as Tomo hit the opposite side wall, followed by a splash as he landed in the creek. A feeble whine echoed out. Finally, having acquired a sufficient quantity of air to speak, Eddie attempted to shout, but it came out as little more than a whisper, "No…" he begged. Eddie received another painful kick in the chest for his efforts.

Cynthia stormed to the ravine. Once again, Eddie found himself unable to draw breath. Despite that, he summoned up every ounce of willpower and strength he had and began dragging himself forward.

Cynthia made her way to the edge of the ravine, since she was taller than it was deep, she hopped down and disregarded the roots Eddie needed to climb down safely. She landed with a heavy splash.

Eddie frantically clawed his way forward, scraping his arms and tearing his shirt in the process. He heard a sharp bark followed by another splash. Immediately after, a thrashing sound began. Eddie made his prone journey at a speed not even a snail would envy. The thrashing and splashing noises continued, every now and then accented with a grunt or a curse.

When Eddie finally reached the edge of the ravine, he just barely managed to peek his head over. Tomo writhed desperately in the creek as Cynthia held the front half of his body underwater, his hind legs clawed at her arms, but with a grunt, she ignored the superficial cuts. The sediments in the creek bed were disturbed by the scuffle, and the crystal-clear water Tomo and Eddie had enjoyed earlier became brown and murky as if the creek itself were attempting to conceal the abominable deed. Moments later, Tomo stopped flailing.

Disregarding his own well-being, Eddie slithered his way over the edge and plopped down into the creek. The tumble left him with several more scrapes and bruises, but he ignored them, his eyes plastered on the motionless lump of wet brown fur setting in the center of the creek. Eddie wanted to deny it, he wanted to believe his eyes were misleading him again. After all, they had failed him just a short while ago, they could be lying to him now. His rent spirit couldn't endure, and Eddie diverted his gaze, unable to maintain an iota of resolve. He would have emptied the contents of his stomach once more if it weren't already void. Instead, he started dry heaving again.

Cynthia stormed away from the scene, too angry at her stupid brother and his stupid dead mutt to linger. She rinsed her cut fingers and torn ankle a couple of dozen yards upstream and struck out for home.

Eddie remained kneeling in the creek for a time, unsure of when or how he found the strength to sit up or even start breathing again. He didn't remember exiting the creek, or even the following days. The considerable spirit and willpower that supported him throughout his early childhood died that day; perished alongside his best friend. Never was a dog possessed of so strong a spirit, it was only natural for Eddie's spirit to follow Tomo to the grave.

– ❂ – Chapter 2 – ❂ –

Edgar Humbert was woken by the rhythmic rapping of hard plastic on metal. He pushed himself up off his stomach to his knees and considered his most recent nightmare, it was more akin to a vivid memory than an impromptu dream. They did that lately. Long gone were the hallucinated horrors and fantasies that graced his mind. Now he dealt only with the poignant and cruelly accurate reminders of his insufficiently suppressed past.

Why must my imagination torture me? Edgar wondered. *The very things I try but fail to forget are reproduced during my only respite from reality.* Edgar's chest tightened, and his breathing became strained; he heaved forward, almost falling prone but catching himself halfway. He remained on his hands and knees for several seconds before he recovered from his latest respiratory failure. Slowly he became aware of the rapping noise again. He turned his head, hands still supporting whatever weight his knees didn't. Standing at his grated door was a clean-shaven young man with short-cropped brown hair under the green uniform cap that matched the color of his freshly creased slacks. His long-sleeved, button-up shirt was tan and similarly creased, with a shiny metal badge displayed over his heart. On his belt dangled a set of comically large keys, along with a radio, two pairs of handcuffs, and an empty pouch. To Edgar, he looked to be no older than 20. The young man wielded a black, heavy plastic baton which he was using to produce the noise that woke Edgar.

"Don't die on us yet," he taunted, his baton falling silent as he began speaking, "It'd be too much of a hassle. Just wait until this evening, much less paperwork if you bite it on our schedule."

Edgar stared at the youthful guard, he didn't recognize him, though he hadn't exactly scrutinized them all or committed their faces to memory. That required effort, something Edgar found scarcer and scarcer since his incarceration. Still, the young man didn't look familiar in the least. A new hire? A transfer? Did it even matter? Edgar realized it didn't.

"It's chow time, old man," the guard announced. "Don't know why we even bother on your last day, especially since you get that fancy meal later, but rules are rules. Maybe I'll change them one day, but for now, that's above my pay-grade, so take your tray and let me finish my rounds." Edgar didn't respond other than to crawl out of the concrete cubby that served as his bed, a bed made barely livable with only a meager foam mattress and a tattered blanket, and sat at the small table near the front of his modest cell. He didn't plan on eating, he seldom did nowadays; he just couldn't bring himself to remain in that cubby, the rookery of his nightmares, any longer.

Edgar looked up, and to his surprise, the young man was still there, an irritated look on his face. The others just slid the tray through the bean-hole in his door and left, but it looked like nobody told the new guy. "What are you, deaf?" he demanded, "somebody went through all the trouble of making you this food, and you're not even going to eat it?" Edgar gave the man his best apologetic look, but, in accordance with everything else Edgar attempted, the look was blank and devoid of any emotion. The guard, made uncomfortable by Edgar's empty gaze, began dragging his baton back and forth across the bars of Edgar's cell again.

"I guess I gotta keep this up until you come get your tray."

Forced out of his mechanical routine by the change of feeding procedure, Edgar forced himself to his feet again. His knees protested, but he didn't want to offend the young man any more than he, unwittingly, already had. Edgar wasn't afraid of anything the guard might do, but he had spent his entire adult life, and the better part of his childhood avoiding conflict, and old habits die hard. When Edgar reached out for the tray, the guard flipped it over and onto the ground. "Keep me waiting at lunch, and you'll have to pick it off the floor too!" he fumed before turning and walking away from Edgar's cell.

Unsure of what to make of the young guard, and unsure whether he even cared, Edgar stooped down and meticulously began cleaning up the splattered foodstuffs. He had to use some of his toilet paper to clean up parts of it, but once everything was back on the tray, he placed it out through the bean hole, careful not to spill it, and sat down once more. Edgar could only sigh as he reminisced about the many other times his attempts at conflict avoidance had yielded poor results.

"What was that about?" the sergeant asked the young man who'd just thrown Edgar Humbert's breakfast on the floor of his cell.

"He took too long to get up," the young man reasoned. "Plus, why does it matter? He'll be in the chair this evening, it's not like he's going to starve or anything. And he's got that last meal coming in, so—"

"Enough," his supervisor interrupted. "It may be your first day on D-Block, but you're still going to be held accountable for your actions. You came here highly recommended, and I refuse to believe what you've shown me today is all you're worth."

"Don't you think you're overreacting?" the young guard accused. "I mean, from what you said earlier, he barely eats anyways. And it's not like he's going to give us any problems. His record says he's not hostile and complies with every order. And he's so skinny and sickly looking, it wouldn't even matter if he tries."

"Have you ever fought a man with nothing to lose?" he asked.

"Most of the prisoners have nothing to lose."

"Have you ever fought a man with a scheduled time to die?" came the grim response. The young man shook his head side to side. "You don't know this man's life, his past, or his thoughts."

"We have his history in the system. And—"

"Interrupt me again, and you'll wish you were the one going in the chair," the sergeant warned. The younger man shrank back. "We have his history, yes. But it doesn't tell us much about him. Sure, he's been anything but trouble his entire stay here, but he could snap at any moment. He's a killer, kid. He's done it before and might try it again. Especially now that he knows his time is almost up…" He paused to let his trainee chew on the words. "A scarier thought, at least in my mind, is, what if he's innocent?"

The kid gave him an incredulous look. "Yes, I know, I've read the files, the evidence was overwhelming. But, when you look at that broken little man, do you really think he would deny the charge, even if it were false?"

The young man thought back to his encounter with Humbert. If he were always this broken, it seemed reasonable, but he'd assumed Humbert had fallen apart while in prison; perhaps prior to his sentencing, but definitely not before the crime, that just didn't make any sense.

"Granted," his sergeant continued, "the possibility is slim to none, I see you rolling the details around in your head. The case is solid, but in the event it's not, poor Humbert not only has to deal with his execution, but also—"

"Has to deal with somebody like me," the young man said contemplatively. The sergeant ignored the interruption and patted his new officer on the back.

"There's that intelligence your recommendation mentioned. I just had to shovel through all the bullshit," he laughed. "Don't worry too much about whether or not he's innocent, it's best to believe everyone on D-Block is guilty, for your own peace of mind. I don't doubt his charges for a second. All the more reason not to rile him up before the final moments. When you escort him to the chair later, the last thing I want to see is a decrepit little man beating on my trainee.”

The young man laughed briefly before catching on to what he was being told. “When *I* escort him?” he asked.

“Yup,” came the casual response. “I believe the best way to learn is to do, first day on D-Block or not; we might as well get it out of the way now while we can. Besides, we don’t know when the next execution will be, could be years, and I’d like to retire knowing everyone on my team knows their stuff.”

The young man beamed. While not overly excited about the execution itself, he was undoubtedly enthusiastic about getting to partake in something so important so soon. A dark thought passed through his mind. “Sir,” he began, “you don’t think he’ll actually put up a fight, do you?”

“I have no idea,” he said. “Don’t know the man, all the more reason to treat him well the last few hours, eh? Now don’t go and pull some Green Mile bullshit on me either. He’s guilty. Don’t question it or feel bad about what we have to do. He made his choices, and now he has to face the consequences. And if you do find yourself questioning it, just remember, this ain’t a Stephen King novel, I don’t care how compliant he is, you let a death row prisoner out of the facility, that sonofabitch ain’t coming back.” With that, he laughed and walked away, leaving the young guard behind, confused, and trying to remember whether or not he’d ever read The Green Mile.

***

The forced memory disturbed Edgar. Of everything his mind could have regurgitated, it had to be Tomo. He crossed his arms and put his head down. Edgar would normally discard the distressing dream, but something made this one linger. Was it the nature of the memory? It was, in a way, the prelude to every other horror he, not so blindly, stumbled into. Or was it his encounter with the new guard? He didn't think something so simple could disrupt the self-inflicted mental desolation he used to cope. Now, memories rushed at him with reckless abandon, jostling his nerves like the turbulence of a squall. *Just a few more hours,* he anguished. *I was so close, why must they appear now?*

After the initial shock of the ordeal, and the psychological lock-down that followed, Edgar had floated along, insensible to everything around him. He was still cognitively aware of his predicament, but he had skirted by emotionally detached. His spirit hadn't been whole for a long time, and after what occurred *that night*, the last pieces skittered away. Edgar was already dead inside; now life was just a formality while he waited for his body to follow suit. Or so he thought. Now, on the very last day, he found that a splinter of his spirit remained; just large enough and lodged just deep enough to cause him grief.

A noise gave Edgar alarm, making him jump back and jerk his head to the side. The young guard from earlier was standing at his door. Caught off-guard by Edgar's uncharacteristic movement, he jumped back as well, suddenly more mindful of his mentor's advice. Seeing the guard's alarm, Edgar attempted once more to put on an apologetic mask. It must have been more convincing than the last one because the guard relaxed a bit.

Confused about the young man's presence, but willing to work with any excuse available to distract his mind, Edgar spoke for the first time in months. "Yes?" it came out a croak, sounding alien to both parties.

The guard studied his face as if looking for something. Several seconds of silence passed, and Edgar found himself about to speak again if only to hear his own strained voice, but the guard overcame his hesitance. "So, you do talk?" he threw out nonchalantly.

The question wasn't asked with any honest interest and was brimming with poorly veiled irritation, but not wanting to be left alone with his thoughts at that moment, Edgar croaked out another, "Yes."

"Well, at least that word," the man quipped, rolling his eyes. "I don't mean to intrude or anything, I can tell you're a very busy man. But you've got me a tad curious about something. Do you mind – or rather, can I ask you some questions? You know, if you don't mind and you're capable of answering."

Not wanting to be probed, but seeing no other way to avoid the suddenly harrowing solitude, Edgar decided that he really didn't have anything to lose by talking to the unpleasant man. The way the guard worded the question though left him unsure of how to answer, and after a small bit of consideration, Edgar realized it probably didn't matter how he responded. For the sake of showing himself capable of saying more than just yes, he let out a third croak, "No."

"Perfect. I appreciate that," the guard said before placing a chair backward in front of Edgar's cell and sitting down with his arms draped over the back, facing Edgar. "Now, before I start, I would like to apologize for my actions earlier. I may have been…" he paused, "…out of line. You see, I'm new to this block, and I mistook your…" another pause, "…melancholy for disobedience. The prisoners on the other blocks, they act differently than you do, and while I don't make it a habit of throwing trays on the ground, I don't let them disrespect me. Understand?" Edgar nodded his head. "Good!" he said cheerfully. "With that unpleasant business out of the way, I guess I can start with my questions. Before I ask, I just want to make sure you're capable of saying more than just yes and no because if you aren't, I'll have to rephrase the questions."

Edgar didn't know what to make of the fast-talking young man, he didn't seem genuine, but he also didn't appear entirely insincere. "What's your name?" Edgar asked, his voice course but beginning to edge back toward his usual tone.

The man looked almost as surprised by the fact that Edgar could talk as he was by the unexpected question. "Officer Cody P. Roach," he said proudly after his surprise dissipated. "You can call me Officer Roach." Usually, Roach wouldn't give out his full name to the prisoners, but since Edgar would be gone tomorrow, he didn't see any harm in it. He opened his mouth to speak again but was halted by Edgar's follow up question.

"How old are you, Officer Roach?"

Disliking being cut off but trying to control himself, Roach answered the question but couldn't resist following it was a snide comment. "Twenty-two. I'd ask your age, but I've been told it is rude to ask the elderly their age." Edgar smiled and chuckled softly. The way Roach talked; he actually did feel like an old man. "So, what's the deal? Why are you here? And don't give me some smart-ass shit like, because we won't let you leave."

Edgar's smile vanished; it wasn't the last comment that chased it off but the question. Edgar hadn't talked about his charges since his trial. Even then he just answered yes to everything, much to the disdain of his attorney. Many of the questions and accusations he confessed to weren't, by technicality, acts he committed, but he was too subdued and guilt-stricken not to feel wholly responsible; so, he accepted the additions as penance, though to him, no amount of punishment would prove sufficient enough to expunge his deeds.

Roach, noticing Edgar's brooding expression, asked, "That bad, huh?" Edgar nodded slowly but didn't move to speak. Several seconds passed before Roach spoke up again. "Well, best get used to me sitting here because I'm not leaving until you start talking." He rested his chin on his arms to show he intended to do just that.

Edgar eased away from his sulking, growing curious about the young man's sudden interest in him and peculiar change in attitude since their initial encounter. With nothing to do and fearing his final hours of solitude, Edgar rasped, "I'm 37." The Roach didn't immediately understand Edgar's words, the confusion showed clearly on his face. When he caught on to which question Edgar was answering his eyes went wide.

"Thirty-seven?" he stammered. Edgar nodded his head in confirmation, a minute grin creasing his face for the first time in months. The young man found himself at a loss for words, amusing Edgar even further. Roach scrutinized the condemned man. Edgar's appearance suggested that he carried with him the weight and burden of several decades of life, perhaps double what he claimed. His pasty sun-starved skin wore many blemishes and sagged from his emaciated frame. His wrinkled filth covered hands shook slightly with what Roach had assumed was arthritis or something akin to it. His wispy black hair, or what remained, was fading and unkempt. His face bore the wrinkles of a stressful life and showed discolored areas Roach had initially thought were liver spots, though now recognized as half-healed patches of acne. Edgar's thin, pale lips were cracked and, in some places, recently split, leaving scattered slivers of red-brown scabs.

Roach hadn't thoroughly examined Edgar earlier, and just now noticing his poor health and hygiene, along with knowing Edgar's age, somehow it made his haggard appearance more pronounced. "Jesus…" he began softly, "you really ought to take better care of yourself." Edgar's throaty laugh caught Roach off guard, and it took him a moment to realize the irony of his statement. Edgar's chest tightened from the uncharacteristic laugh, and it devolved into a coughing fit.

Roach stumbled through a response to recover from his unintentionally cruel words, but Edgar stopped him with a trembling upraised hand. "It's okay." Edgar wheezed. Edgar was too amused at seeing the young man's words catch in his mouth to feel the sting of the previous comment or the rough grating in his throat and chest.

"You spoke out of concern, not malice," he managed between coughs, "I think I'll let it slide…" Edgar paused to control his breathing, caught on his own words. For a fleeting moment, the young man had shown genuine, if misplaced, concern for him.

After Edgar finished trying to expel his lungs from his body, Roach continued. "So how did you end up here and…" He paused, searching for kinder words, but quickly decided they weren't necessary, "…like this?"

Edgar chewed on the question, unsure of where to begin or if he even wanted to open up to this young man. "You've seen my charges?" Edgar asked. Roach nodded. "Well, you know why I'm here then…" He paused, "But I'm guessing you want the story behind it all, right?"

Roach smiled. "Yeah, I'm curious what turns a man into a creature like yourself." Edgar returned his smile, taking no offense at the quip. "But do spare me some of the more…graphic details."

Edgar sat silently for several moments causing Roach to playfully ask, "That hard to clean it up?"

"No," came Edgar's distant response, "I just don't know how to start."

"From the beginning," Roach suggested as if it should have been obvious.

Edgar contemplated the story's true origin. He thought of Tomo. "No," he thought out loud, "that won't do." Roach wore a perplexed expression, but Edgar didn't take note, too preoccupied with sifting through memories. He thought of his ex-wife, his sister, and of course, Annie. "I suppose I could start by telling you the first time I met her." Edgar mused. "When I first met Annie, I—"

"All available officers to C-3-E immediately! All available officers to C-3-E immediately!" Roach's radio blared. Roach bolted so quickly his chair launched forward, smashing into the front of the cell door where Edgar's fingers clung. There was a muted crack as his ring finger broke. Edgar retracted his hands and screamed silently. When Edgar returned his gaze to his cell door, Officer Roach was already gone, responding to whatever emergency had called him away.

A thought crossed Edgar's mind. In all his time on D-Block, he heard the various officers' radios summon all nearby personnel several times, but only for emergencies on D-Block. Roach's radio had said C-3-E, a cell on C-Block. *Was the situation so severe that they needed additional personnel, or did Officer Roach have his radio tuned to listen in to all the channels hoping for more excitement?* Edgar decided it was probably the latter considering what he knew about the brash young man.

By the time Edgar looked back down, his ring finger had already swollen and was beginning to turn purple. He tried to bend it, but pain prevented his attempt. *Definitely broken,* he thought. He figured it didn't matter, he'll fry just the same that evening. He wondered what the repercussions were for abandoning your post and injuring an inmate in the process, albeit a minor injury. Officer Roach would be fired, if not for his actions directly then for causing the lawsuit. At the very least the paperwork for the broken finger would delay his execution until the following Friday since it would take several hours to complete, and that would bring forth questions about the delay, possibly drawing lawyers out claiming abuse or foul play and demanding retribution.

With those thoughts in mind, Edgar knew precisely what he had to do. He had to hide his injury.

While Edgar cared little for Officer Roach, he had no desire to cause any issues for the young man or his employer, and even if he wanted to, he didn't have the guts to do any of it. He also had no desire to continue living, even if only for another week. He would have committed suicide a while back if he'd had the nerve for it. But, like everything else in his life, Edgar just couldn't do it.

***

When Officer Roach returned 15 minutes later, his crisp uniform was soggy, and his neatly combed hair was disheveled. His forehead was rimmed with moisture, and his smile was wide. "Sorry old man," he shouted as he passed Edgar's cell, having apparently forgotten Edgar's age. "Looks like I won't be able to hear your story, I've got one hell of a report to write." And with that, he swaggered off.

When he reached the side of the hallway, Officer Roach was stopped by his supervisor. The older man was talking in a low, hushed tone, affording Roach some privacy, but Roach didn't catch on and spoke loud enough for Edgar to hear his half of the conversation.

"Hello, Sir… There was an incident on C-Block… I was coming back from the bathroom and passed by C-Block when it happened, so I responded… I know, shitty timing… No, I'm fine… I'm actually headed to write my incident report now… What?… No, Sir… I… No, Sir… Yes, Sir… Okay, won't happen again…"

Based on what he heard, Edgar assumed his guess had been correct. Officer Roach had left his post to get involved in an incident outside of his assigned area, and his supervisor knew it. Edgar was drawn away from his thoughts by the approach of Sergeant Lewis, the head of D-Block, and Officer Roach's supervisor. He'd just been walking through but stopped when he noticed the overturned chair in front of Edgar's cell. When Sergeant Lewis shifted his gaze from the chair to Edgar, Edgar instinctively moved to hide his swollen digit under the table.

"Something wrong with your hand, Mr. Humbert?" The perceptive sergeant asked. Edgar shook his head, no. "Why don't you go ahead and pull it from under the table for me then." Hesitantly, Edgar revealed his injured finger, swollen to the size of a walnut now. Sergeant Lewis let out a whistle. "How'd you manage that?"

Edgar paused and searched frantically for an explanation, but after coming up empty, merely shrugged his shoulders.

"I heard a loud smash not too long ago," Sergeant Lewis continued, "Thought maybe you finally lost it and either slammed your head or punched the wall…" He paused and turned his gaze to the chair and back, exaggerating the movement to ensure Edgar noticed. "You don't appear to have lost it. Maybe you're just tired of Roach talking, God knows I am." Edgar stared at him and after a few moments, nodded his head in agreement.

"Very well." Sergeant Lewis said, "I'll have to type up a report, but since the injury was self-inflicted, it'll be brief, and nothing will come of it." Edgar visibly relaxed. "At least, that's what the official documents will say, which I want you to sign just in case. But," he lowered his voice to a whisper, "off the record, I'd like you to tell me something.

How does one injure his ring finger punching a wall, but none of the other fingers?"

Edgar bristled, and Sergeant Lewis laughed. "I appreciate what you're doing for my new officer." Sergeant Lewis said. "I knew he'd need some work when I saw he was transferring from C-Block, don't get me wrong, they do good work there, but D-Block requires a more…subtle approach. We'll get Roach acclimated before long, he's a smart kid, and thanks to your cooperation, he might just last long enough for us to do it."

Edgar's smile was genuine, but whether that was because of the Sergeant's words or just from avoiding conflict, he was unsure.

"One more thing," he continued, "I know you're not big on laughing, but you might just find this humorous." The sergeant looked around and continued in a hushed tone. "Don't tell your pal, Roach, but this corridor has video and audio monitoring devices hidden in it. I watched your whole encounter." With that, Sergeant Lewis laughed and walked away.

Chapter 3

"Eddie, we're getting a divorce," Amy said, her tone offering no room for debate.

Eddie wore an incredulous expression. "But, w…why?" he stammered, his chest beginning to tighten. "This is so… Sudden. Unexpected."

"Unexpected?!" Amy nearly hissed. "Were you born blind Eddie or are you just too afraid to open your eyes?"

"I didn't…" he began with difficulty, his asthma starting its assault.

"Of course, you didn't see anything wrong! You never do! Our marriage has been stale from the start, and you didn't see anything. I've been cheating on you for years, and guess what? You didn't see anything!"

Eddie couldn't draw breath he was so shocked, not that he'd have been able to anyways, his asthma was too intense.

"Nothing to say?" she asked sharply. "Do you see it now?! The late nights at the office, the frequent business trips, the new clothes, the new perfume, the new hairstyle. Were none of these red flags to you?" Eddie had noticed his wife's sudden increased efforts in her appearance but had thought it was because she wanted to look better for him since the increasing demands of her job took so much of their time together away. Looking back, he saw how foolish that was. "Do you remember the last time we had sex?" she asked.

Eddie thought back, it was a couple of weeks ago. He had come home from shopping to find Amy lying on their bed naked, supposedly waiting for him to get back. His eyes shot open at the realization, and he would have gasped if his lunges allowed him.

Noticing the awareness in his eyes, Amy continued, "We were in our bed when you came home, so I had him hide in the closet until you finished. Afterward, I sneaked him out, and we drove to the park where he finished what you couldn't."

On a conscious level, Eddie knew he should have felt angry and betrayed, instead he felt impotent. He hadn't been good enough for Amy, he always thought he didn't deserve her; apparently, she had found out too. And now they were getting a divorce.

Reading the sadness in her husband's eyes, Amy raged, "What kind of a man are you?! I had an affair! I cheated on you! You should be furious! Instead, you look like a chastised puppy! Don't you even want to know who it is?!" Edgar shook his head, no. He really didn't. She tightened her lips and clenched her fists. "Mike," she said through clenched teeth. "It was Mike Bowen."

Eddie's shoulders dropped further. He knew Mike, he was a writer he had worked with in the past. He liked the kid enough but wasn't a huge fan of his work, though it sold well. He was one of those writers who did it for the money, though older writers would tell you most writers won't make much if anything; Mike had been one of the lucky few, mostly due to his willingness to exploit the current fad among young readers to jump on anything vampire or anti-government.

Eddie couldn't help but picture the young man in bed, in *his* bed, with his wife. His beautiful wife Amy, who seemed to stop aging at 25 despite being three years Eddie's senior at 38 years old, sleeping with a man barely old enough to legally drink. A profound sadness swept over Eddie. "I'm sorry," he managed between coughs.

Amy exploded at that, "You're sorry?! I have an affair, and *you're* sorry? You spineless bastard! I can't believe you! Mike is twice the man you are, and he's hardly more than half your age! He even stopped going by Mikey when he realized he was an adult. But you, you're still Eddie! Eddie, who can't notice when his wife is cheating on him. Eddie, who can't find a real job. Eddie, who apologized when his wife confessed to an affair! Eddie, who can't tell anybody 'no' when they ask for something. I bet if I had asked your permission to sleep with Mike, you'd have said *yes!* Maybe it's a good thing we don't have kids because they'd walk all over you too!" Amy was breathing heavily, her face flushed red.

Every word stung, especially the last comment, Eddie always wanted children, and Amy's barrenness had been the only thing he hadn't absolutely loved about her, even now. Despite the sting of her words, he couldn't rebuke any of it. He was beginning to catch his breath, though his chest still hurt. "Edgar then," he said.

Amy's eyes widened, incredulous. "What?" she asked, stern and quiet.

"I'll go by Edgar from now on," he offered.

"That?!" she shouted. "That's what you got from all this?! Do you think that going by Edgar instead of Eddie will make me stay?! Do you even care about the affair?!"

Edgar opened his mouth to respond, but Amy slapped him across the face to silence him. She turned on her heel and walked toward the front door. She opened it and paused, turning her head to regard her soon to be ex-husband. "If I wanted a pussy, I'd have married a woman!" she screamed before leaving and slamming the door.

Edgar had wanted to run after her, to tell her how much he loved her and tell – *tell* not *ask* – her to stay and prove himself a man.

He wanted to but couldn't.

– ❂ – Chapter 4 – ❂ –

The angry roar of thunder woke Edgar from his nap. *What a way to spend my last day,* Edgar mused, *trapped in the prison that is my past.* He guessed it was appropriate. The present was ending, the future was non-existent, what was left but the past. He wished the future would hurry up; he didn't want to relive his past, too many bitter memories. Even the sweet ones tasted rancid because they all eventually soured.

He looked up at the clock. A quarter to three. His last meal was scheduled at three, and his execution at six. The meal he chose was meant to help him leave with good memories, now he knew better. It was too late to change it now. Perhaps he'd just skip dinner.

A streak of lightning danced across the sky followed by the loud drum of thunder its dance birthed. *Of course, there would be a storm,* Edgar lamented, *why wouldn't there be.* He thought back to his conversation with Officer Roach. *Well,* he thought, *I guess I know where I should have begun the story, too late now, always too late…*

"Moping again?" came a familiar voice. Edgar looked up and saw a grinning Officer Roach, a plate of food in his hand. Edgar dismissed the idea of skipping dinner. He didn't think Roach would throw this meal on the floor, but Edgar didn't want to hear the young man complain about him skipping a meal that was *actually* made just for him.

"Here's your pineapple juice and..." Roach paused, inspecting the plate. "Oatmeal cookies?" He crinkled his nose.

"Coconut," Edgar corrected.

"That's even worse," Roach complained. "I'm not a big fan of cookies myself, but coconut has got to be the worst."

"I agree," Edgar said, drawing a perplexed look from Roach.

"Then why did you request them for your last meal?" came the obvious question.

"Coconut cookies have sentimental value to me. I'd explain, but it ties in with the entire story. There wouldn't be time."

"That's a shame. You probably could have written it down for me if we thought of it earlier." Edgar didn't think he'd have had enough time to put it all on paper, but he nodded anyway.

More lightning tore through the dark sky, accompanied by another, much louder, wave of thunder. Roach jumped, spilling a few drops of juice before cursing angrily to himself. "I can't fucking stand thunderstorms!" He handed the paper plate of cookies and the Styrofoam cup of juice to Edgar to avoid spilling them in the event more thunder appeared to rob him of his balance.

"You know..." Roach continued, sounding contemplative, "it'd really be something if the weather made them postpone the chair. The forecast did mention a tropical storm, but I doubt it matters, I mean, what's the worst that could happen? You get electrocuted?" Roach laughed. "I can see the headlines now. Death row prisoner dies preemptively when struck by lightning while strapped in the electric chair! God said this one was his to take!" Roach buckled over laughing, gripping the bars of Edgar's cell to support himself. For just a moment Edgar thought about how easy it'd be to break Roach's fingers but quickly discarded the thought, knowing how truly unlike him that would be. He'd never hurt somebody out of malice, but, he knew all too well there were plenty of other ways to hurt people. His chest itched as if the thought alone might cause an asthma attack.

"But before you start hoping for a delay," Roach continued after catching his breath, "just know you won't get a second last meal. Speaking of which, I'll leave you to enjoy your first, and only, last meal in peace." With that, Officer Roach walked away. Outside, the siblings lightning and thunder made themselves known.

***

"Anybody ever told you that you talk too much?" Sergeant Lewis asked.

"On occasion," Officer Roach replied, "but mostly I'm told I should have been a comedian."

"Well, Mr. Comedian, I'm willing to bet that you'll soon regret the last joke you made to Mr. Humbert there."

"Why's that?"

"Because I just got word that his execution will be postponed because of the weather and that he won't be receiving a second last meal."

Officer Roach, for once, found himself speechless.

"I've already tried to change that last fact, even if I can do nothing about the delay, but it's over my head. And since I've put you in charge of his execution ceremonies, you get to be the lucky S.O.B. to tell him the good news."

"Well, fuck me…" Roach said.

***

Edgar stared at the meal in front of him. A dozen warm coconut cookies accompanied by a tall cup of cool pineapple juice. He exhaled, almost sobbing. His breath kissed the cookies before rebounding back to him. The smell made him cringe. Edgar hadn't noticed that his breath mimicked the aroma of a corpse and assumed he hadn't noticed because he must have gradually adjusted to it as the bacteria festered in his mouth. He wondered briefly how long it'd been that way, the only reason he noticed now was because of how starkly it contrasted with his meal.

He lifted a cookie to his cracked lips and took a small bite. He chewed slowly and deliberately, tossing the chunks around his mouth with his tongue, savoring every minute flavor the sugary treat had to offer. After masticating for an eternity, Edgar forced himself to swallow before returning the cookie to the plate for a reunion with its brothers.

Edgar turned his attention to the pineapple juice, it stared him down, daring him to partake in its bitter goodness. Edgar wouldn't take that dare. Already the smell and taste of the cookies were overwhelming his sensibilities, making him wallow in the trauma of his past.

A flash of light illuminated his cell momentarily before the thunder gave it a good shake; the lights flickered. Edgar started crying at the sound. He dropped his face into his filth covered hands, muddy tears streamed through his fingers. *This is where it all began,* he reminisced, *a stormy night with a plate of coconut cookies and a glass of pineapple juice.* The memories tore through his conscience like a cruel storm and Edgar sobbed more fiercely.

Officer Roach's voice interrupted Edgar's moment of self-pity, Edgar shifted his gaze. "So," the young guard began, "remember when I said they wouldn't postpone your execution? Well, the weather's gotten worse, it's now categorized as a tropical storm, and it turns out, they don't want to risk a premature electrocution. And the comment I made about not getting a second last meal, it turns out that my jest was more accurate than I intended it to be. My Sergeant tried to fight it, but that decision is above his station." Edgar stared at Roach, using every last bit of effort he could muster to prevent himself from breaking down. While it was unfortunate that he wouldn't receive another last meal, he was far more distraught over the delay. All executions took place on Fridays. Edgar would have to wait an entire week.

Mistaking Edgar's silence for contempt, Roach asked, "Is there anything I can get you?"

Edgar thought hard on that. He would be trapped in the machinations of his mind for a week. Seven whole days of being thrown into the past and then being brought back to his cell to suffer with it. Edgar thought it appropriate that a monster such as himself would have to deal with such a punishment. He didn't deserve an easy death.

"Nothing?" Roach asked, growing impatient.

On a whim, Edgar asked, "Still want me to write down my story for you?"

Roach's eyes widened slightly. "Sure, I suppose you do have the time for it now." With that, Roach wandered off. A few minutes later he returned with a notebook and a couple of pencils. Edgar thanked him, and Roach left him alone.

For months, Edgar had been labeled a monster, and he had wholeheartedly agreed, but the recent rush of memories left him feeling, in addition to everything else, contemplative. Where did it all go wrong? Was all the blame truly his? He had no doubt the latter question would still be yes, but he had nothing to lose by putting it all down on paper. Perhaps it could even help him cope with the extra time he suddenly had.

Could the words on the page help him find shelter from the internal storm raging in his mind and heart? And if it did, would it be enough to weather it in its entirety?

Pushing those worries aside and steeling his nerves, Edgar settled down to begin. Knowing it would be a lengthy ordeal, Edgar ate a cookie for the caloric boost and washed it down with a swallow of pineapple juice, it didn't taste quite as horrid as the first bite, but it was still difficult to stomach. Content with his decision, Edgar touch pencil to paper and began writing.

– ⊛ – Chapter 5 – ⊛ –

My life had been sluggish and uneventful the year after my divorce. The weeks immediately following it were a hurricane of emotional turmoil and strife; during that time, I was wracked with insomnia and nightmares. I dealt with the former by picking up a new prescription, which only made the latter issue worse, along with adding an occasional bout of sleepwalking. At first, it wasn't a huge problem, I wandered around while sleeping, maybe wake up in a different room or move some insignificant trinket. Those things I could deal with, what I couldn't deal with was the bruised ribs and broken arm from my fall down the stairs.

I stopped taking the pills after that and was eventually able to cope with the insomnia from sheer chronic fatigue. It wasn't the best quality of sleep, I was woken by nightmares which usually ended with an asthma attack. I managed between four and six hours of sleep a night and floated along for months in a cool, comfortable depression.

The changes first occurred when I received a phone call from an unknown number. Initially, I thought it'd be another telemarketer trying to sell me some insurance I didn't need, and quite possibly already had, but would no doubt still end up buying. "No" was a difficult word for me to use. My wife was in the habit of answering the phone if we didn't recognize the number. My first instinct was to call out, "Amy! Telephone!" but I caught myself after the first syllable, remembering her absence.

Unsurprisingly, my chest began to tighten in the starting throes of asthma – they were triggered very easily at this point. I held my breath momentarily and picked up the phone. "Hello? Eddie?" It was a woman's voice that I recognized despite not having heard it in 12 years.

"Cynthia?" I asked, shocked.

"Yeah!" came her cheerful answer. "How's my favorite little brother doing?" It was one of those comments people made when there was no competition for the favorite. Anything for my *favorite* [only] grandchild. Where's my *favorite* [only] daughter? Why hasn't my *favorite* [only] son called me?

"I'm fine," came my automated response.

"Good to hear, how's Amy?"

I'd forgotten Cynthia was still around when Amy and I got married. "I don't know," I lied.

"You don't know?" Cynthia asked, incredulous. "How do you not know how your wife is doing?"

"We got a divorce, Cynthia, about a year ago."

"Oh, really? How sad. It was probably for the best though. I never did like that bitch, she always took advantage of you, Eddie. You were too nice." I wanted to snap back at the hypocrisy of her comment and find some way to defend my beloved wife, ex-wife, whom I – still – loved, but Cynthia spoke the truth, I was too nice.

"You're probably right," I agreed.

"No *probably* about it. But don't worry, I ended up divorced too! I guess it runs in the family. That's why I'm calling. Do you still live in that house or did the leech take that too?"

"I still have Dad's house." Mike, Amy's new husband, and boyfriend at the time of the divorce, lived in a beachfront house, not as large as the two-story five-bedroom house I inherited from my father, but much more beautiful, and *much* more expensive. There was no need for Amy to try and fight me for it, not that I would have put up much of a fight, if I put up any at all. I think Amy knew that and didn't want to take that from me too, bless that woman. It was also the last thing I had left of my father; before he committed suicide, he left it to me in his will for when I turned 18, it made sense he'd skip the wife that left him – I guess it does run in the family.

"Why do you ask?" I said, worried she was looking to stay in one of my spare bedrooms.

"Well, since I left my good for nothing husband, I figured you'd let me stay in one of your rooms."

"Of course," I said.

"I'm just kidding, Eddie." She laughed, "You really are too nice. Actually, I bought a place on your street a few houses down. We'll be neighbors!" I blew an internal sigh of relief. "Besides, I don't want my daughter to grow up squatting at my brother's place, she might not grow up independent and think it's okay to completely rely on others, can't have that."

"You have a daughter?"

"Of course. I was married about as long as you were. Don't tell me you don't have a few of the little gremlins running around."

"Actually, Amy was barren," I said, slightly distraught.

"Oh…" She paused. "All the better you left her." I didn't bother to correct Cynthia about who left who.

"It's a good plan," I said, jumping backward in the conversation. "I think it's good for a child to grow up independent. That's a very mature decision. If you ever need anything, give me a call or just come knocking." I partially regretted saying it, knowing she'd more than likely take me up on that offer, but Cynthia would probably ask for favors whether I offered or not.

"Oh, Eddie," she said, sounding hurt, "I hope you don't think I'm the same reckless person I was in my youth. I've grown up, it just took me longer than it should have. I have so many regrets, but now I just want to do what's best for my daughter and do right by the family, what's left of it at least."

I realized that I had assumed she was the same as in her youth, and that was unfair of me. "I'm sorry," I said, "it has been a long time since we've seen each other. I'm sure we've both grown a lot, we should catch up once you're moved in."

"We should," she said. "I wonder how my little Eddie has changed."

"Well," I said, slightly cheerful, "I go by Edgar now."

"Your wife's doing?"

"How'd you know?"

"Because I know my little brother Eddie," she chuckled. "Don't worry though, if you go by Edgar now, then that's what I'll call you!"

"I appreciate that."

"No problem. Anyway, I'll be moving in this week. I can't wait to see you!"

"Same here," I said. After that, we said our *goodbyes* and hung up. My sister and I had a complicated childhood with our parents getting divorced and our dad committing suicide, on top of that, our personal relationship was strained at the best of times, but people grow up, after all, it had been 12 years since I last saw Cynthia. Besides, we had both recently gone through divorces, we could help each other cope, though she seemed to be dealing with hers better than I was mine.

Twelve years ago, I was almost a year into my own marriage when Cynthia got married and moved away. At the time, I was 23 and Cynthia was 28. Ever since she left, she was kicked out of our mother's home at 19, she jumped from job to job, from apartment to apartment, and party to party. She always had a drinking problem, that was part of the reason Mom kicked her out. She was an intelligent woman, but reckless to a fault. Mom was honestly surprised she never got knocked up as a teen or in an alcohol-related car accident. She was bold, confrontational, and refused to take "no" for an answer. Last I saw her, she was thin and mildly pretty; she was a large child and preteen though, so that could have easily changed in 12 years. I never met her husband, he lived out of state, and she moved in with him while they were dating and never bothered to introduce him to us. She wasn't the perfect sister, but then again, nobody's perfect. I found myself looking forward to our reunion.

***

About a week later, Cynthia came knocking at my door. As soon as I opened it, she wrapped me in a hug. "It's been far too long!" she said. I agreed and invited her inside. She grabbed a bottle of wine off the ground she'd sat down in preparation for the hug and followed me in.

My house was sparsely decorated and under-furnished since it had far more room than I had furniture to fill it with. Cynthia commented on that fact as I directed her to the dining room.

"There was more before Amy left, but most of the furniture was hers since she was in charge of decorating. Even then it was still spacious. Now it just feels empty." The double meaning of my last comment was lost on Cynthia.

"No kidding," Cynthia said, inspecting the bare walls and barren hallways on the way towards the dining room. "Well, nothing to do now but celebrate."

"Celebrate?" I asked as we reached our destination.

"Celebrate the separations of our marriages and the rejoining of our family," she said, hoisting the wine bottle in the air.

"Sounds good, but I'm not much of a drinker."

"Nonsense," Cynthia said, digging through my cabinets on a hunt for a couple of glasses. "We're not getting wasted Eddie, sorry, Edgar, we're just celebrating our long-overdue reunion. Ah-ha!" she said, pulling two decorative wine glasses from the depths of storage. They were the wine glasses Amy and I used on our honeymoon, I'd forgotten they were in there, Amy must have either forgotten about them too or chose to leave them to avoid remembering me. I didn't feel comfortable drinking out of them but couldn't bring myself to say anything to Cynthia.

She set the glasses on the table and filled them each a little over halfway. She passed me one and raised hers in a toast. "To family." We tapped the edges of our glasses together, and each took a sip, though Cynthia's sip looked strangely like a series of swallows and left her glass drained.

"I'm sorry," Cynthia said, reading my face. "I know what it must look like. Alcoholic sister leaves for a decade with a man nobody met and when she comes back, the first thing she does is start drinking." I didn't say anything, and she took that as her queue to continue. "I, at some point along the way, realized I had a problem, sadly that moment is far closer to the present day than the day I left; since then I've started making progress. But the divorce stressed me out, and the move, and raising my daughter alone. It's been rough Edgar…" She paused and put her hand on mine. "But, now I'm back. I know we've never been buddy-buddy, and I know I've done some pretty terrible things in the past…" She paused as I winced. "But I want to make things right. I want to be there for my family, I missed your wedding, I didn't invite you to mine," she swallowed, "I missed Mom's funeral. You're the only real family I have left. You and Annie. And I want to be there for you both."

I tried to respond but stopped myself for fear I'd break down and start crying, Cynthia however, held no such reservations and began crying herself. "I've changed Edgar, and I want to keep changing. I've been falling back into old habits because of all the drama, but it won't be for long. I need your help to make myself a better person. For me, and for Annie. Will you help me do that? Please?"

At that, I did tear up. "Of course, I will," I said, embracing my sister in a hug. "We're family, it's never too late to start acting like one." In the family, I'd always been the crybaby. I can't remember a single time she legitimately cried before that moment; but there we were, holding each other and squealing like newborns. She cried for me, for herself, for Mom, and for her daughter; I cried for her, for Dad, and for Amy. We poured our hearts into those tears and let them pool together. Finally, a family.

Chapter 6

Edgar put his second pencil down, the points were both flat. He looked at the clock, a few hours had passed, yet the storm continued its tantrum. He wore the pencils down so thoroughly that the last several lines he'd written were comprised of fat crooked letters. He planned on getting Roach's attention to sharpen them for him, but he'd been absent since Edgar started writing. He'd only recently reappeared, convenient since the pencils were almost unusable.

"Officer Roach," Edgar asked, "can you sharpen these pencils for me?"

Roach grabbed the pair of pencils and nodded noncommittally before pausing and taking note of the many pages Edgar had penned. "I didn't plan on reading a novel. How much more do you have to add?"

Edgar shrugged, unsure of the final length. "I don't know," Edgar said in all seriousness, "I guess I'll keep going until it's done."

"Well, I guess you have plenty of time now," Roach said before leaving, unaware of the pain Edgar felt because of his unexpected bonus week of life. The comment itself reminded Edgar of that fact, reopening the recent wound, but with uncharacteristic willpower, he ignored it, knowing he was about to dive further into his memories, reopening much older, and much deeper, wounds. Dwelling on his want, and temporary denial, of death, would compromise his resolve to finish the task at hand.

The pause in writing made Edgar aware of his hunger, he choked down a couple more cookies and another swallow of juice. His hunger did nothing to improve the taste, but he managed to keep it all down.

Edgar waited several minutes, but Roach hadn't returned yet. He stared out the window to distract himself, but the squall outside too directly mirrored the internal one wracking him. He shifted his gaze to the polished aluminum plate on the wall that served as a mirror.

He'd seen his reflection recently but hadn't truly looked at himself. He did so now and didn't like what he saw. Edgar realized Roach really couldn't be blamed for mistaking his age. Edgar washed his face and hands the best he could, then cupped water in his hands and filled his mouth with it. He swished, gargled, and spat. It wasn't much, but he felt refreshed; it also helped remove the bitter aftertaste from the pineapple juice and evict the last stubborn crumbs left by the cookies.

"You really should have chosen a different meal," Roach said from outside the bars of Edgar's cell. "I mean, if you feel the need to rinse your mouth out after eating them, it was probably a poor choice, nostalgia aside."

Edgar smiled at Officer Roach's unrelenting jests. "They're not as bad as I thought they'd be," Edgar lied, "I only wish I'd have them for my actual last meal."

Roach winced, having taken Edgar's comment seriously. "Here are your pencils back," he said holding his hand out, "and also a pen, my shift is about over, and I can't promise other officers will sharpen them for you."

Edgar thanked him and took the trio of writing utensils from Officer Roach. The pen was short, less than four inches long, flexible to prevent it from being converted into a shank, and, save for the ink cartridge inside, completely transparent. It dawned on Edgar that the pencils themselves were contraband, potentially dangerous in and of themselves. He began to wonder about the prudence of Officer Roach's generosity. In the wrong hands, pencils were a weapon, so none of the prisoners were permitted access to them. Roach was putting himself at risk giving Edgar pencils, not a physical risk from Edgar, he would never attempt such a thing, but Roach could potentially get in trouble for his kindness.

"I really appreciate this," Edgar said, thanking him for more than just the writing utensils.

"Don't mention it, old-timer," came the – feigned – nonchalant response, and for Roach's sake, Edgar intended not to. He had found a new respect for the young Officer Cody P. Roach.

Edgar laid the pen and pencils down and grabbed a couple more cookies to chew on. The weather outside retained its previous intensity, but the storm inside was picking up. Resupplied, Edgar wielded his tools and continued to work on what, he hoped, would protect him from the approaching torrent.

Chapter 7

When Cynthia left, she agreed to leave the bottle of wine with me to help limit the temptation and to save for future celebrations. She said she couldn't wait to introduce me to her daughter Annie and promised to bring her over that upcoming Friday. She said they wouldn't be able to stay for more than a few minutes because she had to go out of town that weekend and needed to find a place for Annie to stay. Naturally, I offered to keep her for the weekend and Cynthia was so grateful she kissed my cheek and wrapped me in one last great hug before leaving.

When Friday rolled around, the sky was overcast with clouds, and a heavy storm was scheduled to hit. No rain had started falling yet, but I could hear distant thunder. I almost missed the knock at my door when it finally came. I answered it and saw Cynthia standing there with Annie. Cynthia never mentioned how old Annie was, in my head I pictured an infant or toddler, but the girl standing behind my sister looked 12, or at the very least nine or ten – I later clarified that Annie was 11 so my guess was nearly on point.

"This is my daughter, Annie," Cynthia said, gently pushing the girl forward. Her appearance caught me off guard, she hardly looked like my sister at all, especially when Cynthia was that age. Annie was on the shorter side, with large emeralds for eyes that showed she was more than a little shy. Freckles spotted the pale skin of her button nose and dimpled cheeks, and her vibrant orange hair was tied up in a ponytail that dangled halfway down her back. She must have been the cutest child I had ever seen – Annie must take after her father because none of these traits were present in my blonde weasel-faced sister. I tried to picture an older male version of Annie but couldn't put it together in my head.

"Say *hi* to Uncle Eddie," Cynthia prompted. Annie gave a brief greeting in the form of a wave. I returned her greeting and Cynthia ushered Annie inside, requesting a moment for the adults to speak. Once she was out of earshot, Cynthia began again, "I know I just got back, and you're already helping me by watching Annie, which you have no idea how much I appreciate, but I need to ask you for a big, big favor."

"Ask away."

"Well, I've been working in sales, and this weekend I was headed out of state to meet some of the higher-ups in the company; if I impress them, I could get a sweet gig. But I left all my suits at my ex-husband's house, and he lives out of state in the opposite direction, and I don't have time to get them. I had planned on buying a new one, but the movers charged me extra because they had to make a second trip. Could you possibly give me a loan, please? I really need to impress these guys."

"How much do you need?" I asked, mentally counting the cash I had on hand.

"The suit I had fitted and altered was 180 dollars. After tax, it'll probably be just under 200."

"Sure thing." I pulled out my wallet and handed Cynthia 200s. I wasn't loaded by any means – 200 dollars was still 200 dollars! – I just did so little with my free-time since Amy left that I started accumulating excess. I didn't have any real hobbies, I just stayed in and read books. I had actually dedicated an entire spare bedroom to a library and study – it was the only room I had that could be considered adequately furnished. I didn't even leave my house to get new reading material, I ordered all of my books online now. I ended up making a small business out of it by writing reviews on a website I threw together, it was popular enough for me to make a living through advertisements, but I lived very frugally, so it wasn't a difficult thing to do. The 200 dollars represented a sizable portion of my weekly income, but better for it to be used helping family then weighing down my wallet.

"Thank you so much!" Cynthia said, her face shifting from desperation to gratitude. "I'll pay you back soon, I promise!" She hugged me and departed, stopping at her car to wave bye to Annie and me.

I closed the door after waving back and turned to see Annie standing at the edge of the room, out of hearing range but still within line of sight. She stood there as if awaiting further instructions. We stared at each other, and it struck me that I had no idea what I was supposed to do with a child for an entire weekend.

I offered her a seat – thinking that the first thing I should do is end the staring contest we started – and with mechanical obedience, she took one. I sat down in the recliner opposite her. I made several attempts to start a conversation, but each time the words died on my tongue.

Annie likewise didn't start a conversation, though probably for lack of trying. She just sat there and stared at me as if she were waiting for some queue to talk or move. The only noise was that of the rain outside as the storm picked up.

Ten minutes in, I suffered a minor asthma attack, which I dealt with silently; the nervousness was getting to me. Annie's nervousness was increasing as well, she was wringing her fingers together but maintained that awkward eye contact. By the time I got my respiratory tract back on track, I allowed my mind to wander, too much focus would help propagate the nervousness. I knew I should probably find some way to break the silence, but the idea of being the one to start the conversation terrified me. *Why did this girl have to be as shy as me?!*

The silence didn't break for half an hour, and it took a force of nature to do it. The storm attacked with a bellow of thunder so fierce the lights flickered. Annie let out a stifled scream at the noise, which came out as barely more than a squeak. It was so adorable I began laughing. *Laughing!* It'd been over a year since I last laughed. Annie pouted, her cheeks flushed red as she said the first four words I ever heard her say. "It's not funny mister."

Somehow, that brief encounter dismissed my anxiety, and I found some of the words that escaped me. "Are you hungry?" I asked, unsure of what girls her age ate or what my sister was feeding her. Annie perked up at the mention of food and nodded her head. I felt a flush of shame as I came to the realization that I had mentally correlated my niece to that of a dog that had to be fed. She was a girl, I could simply ask her what she wanted to eat.

I asked her preference, and she opened her mouth to answer but quickly shut it as if worried about her decision. After a little prodding, she finally whispered, "Coconut cookies?" Never had I kept those foul things in my house.

"I'm sorry," I said, "I don't have any coconut cookies." She immediately deflated and I nearly panicked. Had I just condemned us to silence again? "But, if you really want some, I suppose we could go to the store."

She beamed and grew in confidence at the suggestion. "D-do you think we could pick up some pineapple juice too?" She was two for snacks I couldn't stand, but nonetheless, *no* wasn't in my vocabulary.

The drive to the store was made moderately unsettling because of both the weather and Annie's silent nervousness because of it. Fortunately, it was a short trip, and we arrived without incident. She didn't speak much at the store, other than to tell me which cookies were "the best!" and which ones were "not the best." Eventually, she grabbed a tube of cookie dough she determined was "the very best."

As we walked through the store, she remained close at my side, flinching at every flash of lightning and jumping after each peal of thunder. One particular clap roared so loudly that Annie hugged my waist. I let out a small chuckle, which Annie traded for a pout. I placed my hand on her head as a comforting gesture; initially, she recoiled at the touch, but visibly relaxed when she looked up and saw the warm expression on my face. At the time, I thought nothing of it.

***

After we got back from the store, I set to making the cookies, pulling out a seldom-used cookie sheet and knife. Annie stared wide-eyed as I sliced the tube of dough and placed the chunks in the oven. She was so focused, I thought those green eyes of her would pop right out of her skull.

My gawking was interrupted as Annie asked, "How long will it take, Mister?" When I told her 20 minutes, her eyes opened even wider than before.

"Twenty minutes?!" she wailed, "But that's too long!"

"It'll be quicker if you distract yourself with something, maybe a game?" I offered.

She brightened, "I like games," came her response. "What games do you play?"

"I don't really play them much, but I have a few board games you may like. Clue, Monopoly, Catan, and a few card games like Uno and Skip-Bo. I probably also have a set of dominoes somewhere too."

"Do you have chutes and ladders?" she asked. It just occurred to me I'd listed off a bunch of games she probably too young to understand. I shook my head. "Darn," she said, "I like that one."

"I'm sorry," I said.

"Don't worry, just pick your favorite and teach me how to play!" she suggested.

I thought about it, Monopoly was probably my favorite of the ones I listed, but I doubted she'd get it. "I don't know if I have a favorite," I told her. "I don't really play them."

"Why do you have them then?"

"Amy liked them."

"Who's Amy?"

I paused, realizing I had inadvertently set a trap for myself. "… She was my wife."

"I didn't know you have a wife."

"I don't. Not anymore at least. She's gone."

"That's sad," Annie said, picking up on my souring mood.

"Don't worry," I said, feigning nonchalance, "she always beat me at them anyways. Maybe today I can finally win."

Annie smiled wickedly. "Don't count on it, Uncle Ed!"

***

We were halfway through our second game of Uno, the first a practice so she could pick up on the rules when the timer for the cookies began screaming. Annie showed intense concentration during the game, but as soon as the timer whined, she discarded it, along with the cards in her hand. She excavated herself from the table so quickly that I jumped in surprise. She peered into the oven before turning her gaze on me, wondering why I was still sitting down when the cookies needed to be rescued from the oven. I took the queue and donned oven mitts. Annie looked like she was about to jump out of her skin she was so excited. When at last my mitted paws withdrew the treats from their incubator, her round emeralds nearly doubled in size.

She remained stationary, awaiting my command to spring. I tilted the pan forward and nodded to her. Lightning fast, she snagged a cookie and immediately set about its demise, biting it in half. If the heat bothered her at all, she didn't show it, too entranced by its flavors. I set the tray down and retrieved a glass to pour her some juice. By the time I handed it to her, she'd already murdered another cookie and had kidnapped a third. She attempted to drown this one in the juice but was forced to rip it in two to make it fit. The final three victims died in a similar manner as the third before she washed away the evidence with the remainder of the pineapple juice. The only trace of the crime was a dirty baking sheet and a few soggy crumbs at the bottom of her glass.

"Hungry?" I teased, genuinely shocked at how expeditiously she ravaged half a dozen steaming cookies.

"Not anymore," she smiled, patting her belly. She let out a noise that sounded like a hiccup, but that she excused as a burp, before sitting back down at the table and picking up her hand of cards, her absolute focus returning.

I had the sudden feeling that if she handled the card game with the same intense efficiency as she did the cookies, I might find myself losing frequently.

***

A week later, the singsong alarm of my doorbell heralded Cynthia's arrival. I hadn't been expecting her, but I didn't mind an unannounced visit, the house was dreadfully devoid of life. When I answered, I was met with a quiet, but significantly less nervous, Annie with Cynthia standing behind her, her hands on Annie's shoulders.

"Sorry to bug you again," my sister said, "but I've got good news to share, and I have to ask another favor of you." I nodded for her to go ahead. "You'll be happy to know that I got the gig. I'll be traveling every weekend, but I haven't had time to find a sitter because they just told me yesterday. Would you mind watching my little Annie this weekend? I'll be back on Sunday. Please, Edgar?" It was at that moment I noticed Annie was wearing a backpack, a soft-looking green thing in the shape of a turtle. It was stuffed with what I assumed to be spare clothes and toiletries.

"Of course, she can stay here," I answered, "I'll try to make her as comfortable as possible."

"Thank you so much!" Cynthia said, "Run along now," she told Annie as she ushered her along with a pat on the back. Annie disappeared behind me. "One more thing," Cynthia added. "Since I've been busy trying to get this contract and moving, I haven't been able to work much, so my paycheck was pretty weak. I know you just loaned me some money last week, but I don't have enough gas to get where I'm going. They'll reimburse me once I get there, and when I get back, I can repay you."

"Not a problem, Sis. I don't have any issues helping you get back on your feet. How much do you need?"

"I think 50 will get me there." I handed Cynthia a pair of 20s and a ten, she beamed and hugged me fiercely, thanking me all the while.

When Cynthia left, and I turned around, I was surprised to see that Annie was not patiently waiting just out of earshot like last week, she'd wandered off. "Annie?" I called, "where did you go?"

"The kitchen," came her cheerful response. When I entered the kitchen, Annie was sitting on the counter drinking a glass of pineapple juice. Her head barely came over the counter so she must have had to climb to get up there. It struck me as queer that she had been able to reach the juice. The shelves in the fridge wouldn't support the weight of an 11-year-old girl, even one as tiny as Annie, and the juice was on the top shelf, far beyond her reach.

"How did you reach the juice?" I asked her. She didn't answer, just smiled wide, showing all of her sparkling teeth, and hopped off of the counter. I never found out how she got the juice off the top shelf.

"So what game are we going to play today?" she asked, ignoring my question.

I shrugged. "I could show you all the games, and you could choose for yourself," I offered. "Maybe one of them will catch your eye." She agreed, and I led her to the den, where all the games were stuffed in a closet.

I started to pull the various colorful boxes off their shelves so she could see them, but as I did, she asked, "What's that table for at the bottom?" I gazed down and saw the checkered marble tabletop of my father's old chessboard.

"It's chess," I told her.

"Is it a game?"

"Yes, but—"

"Can you teach me how to play?" she pleaded.

"I suppose I can, but it's pretty difficult. There's a lot of rules to learn before you start playing. Are you sure?"

"Yeah!" she cheered, "Besides, I'm a fast learner."

"We'll see about that," I said, pulling the hefty table out. It was an extravagant piece, made entirely of marble including the pedestal that served as its base. I set it in the middle of the room, Annie opened her mouth, I assumed to ask a question but shut it when I slid the built-in drawers open, revealing the expertly carved and impressively shiny figurines. Her eyes went so wide I thought they would pop right out of her skull.

"They're so pretty," she said in awe, picking up a knight. "Can I be this one?" she asked, holding it towards me.

"This isn't your normal board game," I told her. "You don't play as one piece, you play as 16."

"Sixteen?" she said incredulous, concern creeping its way into her features.

"It's not too late to pick something easier."

All concern and incredulity fled her face and was replaced tenfold with determination. "No, teach me this."

***

A couple of hours passed with Annie's concentration only lapsing when she stopped to cook the remainder of the cookie dough and then once more to eat them; I, once again, did not partake and sated my complaining stomach with an overripe banana.

The fierce concentration Annie had during our card game the previous week was applied to chess twice over. Her brow was furrowed, and her tongue was peeking out the left side of her mouth. She kneeled in her chair, her spindly arms out straight as she leaned on the chess table. We were on our third game, the first, once again, little more than a demonstration of the rules and the second her attempt to solidify them in her mind. On the third game, she had little to no technical errors in her play, apparently having memorized all the rules after just two games. She didn't use any complex strategies, but she did seem to have a firm understanding that she needed to avoid losing her pieces and try to take mine to win.

She lost that game and the next one too; her face reddened more with each consecutive loss. She was growing frustrated, so I started going easy on her; nothing overt, just letting her take a piece every now and then so we'd have roughly the same number of pieces. I'd decided to let her win, but she had difficulty setting up a checkmate, and the game ended in a stalemate. We played one more, and like the previous game, I avoided taking too big of a lead but won to avoid giving the appearance of taking it easy – I had a feeling she wouldn't like that. In the sixth game, I gave away pieces as I had in the previous two. Annie was beginning to think for more extended periods between moves. This game had already gone on for twice as long as the second or third and, by my estimate, we were only halfway through.

I looked out the window, the sky had grown dark over an hour ago, and the stars had come out to play. I glanced at my watch, 15 minutes had passed since the last move. I made a show of yawning, drawing Annie from her contemplation. "It's getting late," I said. "Why don't we pick this up in the morning?"

Annie's face was one of incredulity as if it were absurd to stop midgame, she opened her mouth to say something but stopped to consider my words. Her concentration left her and was replaced with fatigue. She'd been so focused all evening she hadn't even known how tired she was until that focus came to an end. She yawned. "Okay," she said and rubbed her eyes.

I led Annie upstairs to the guest bedroom and tucked her into bed. She fell asleep before I left the room, but I returned a few minutes later and left a glass of water on the nightstand beside the bed. I imagined that if she woke up thirsty, she'd appreciate not having to wander around a darkened house looking for water. Afterward, I retired to my own room and slept.

***

I turned my head and looked at the clock. Five-thirty in the morning, which meant I got six hours of sleep – more than I usually got. I strolled to the kitchen, grabbed some ground coffee beans, and made my way to my office.

My office was a lazy little room without much in it. A desk, a chair, a bookshelf, a computer, and of course, the coffee maker. It seems odd to some to have a coffee maker anywhere else besides the kitchen, but I took pleasure in the little things, like reading a book with the smell of coffee slowly pervading my nostrils. Unlike my library and study, my office contained only one bookshelf. I used one of the largest rooms for the library since I kept the majority of my books there, and just moved the work-related ones to my office. I found that separating my work and leisure reading rooms kept me from growing bored of reading and ensured I didn't get too distracted when it came time to work.

I started the machine and grabbed the latest book by some recently famous young author. I wasn't a fan of his work, but I had to review every popular new release to keep the site going; I think this one was something about the government, or the multiverse, hard to be sure with this guy.

Less than an hour in, I heard the stairs creak and knew Annie was awake. I put the trash novel down and greeted Annie in the kitchen. I inquired about her preference for breakfast and wound up making scrambled eggs and bacon. I sat down, sipping on my coffee as she nibbled on a piece of bacon.

We sat in silence for a time, and I nearly spilled my beverage when Annie abruptly shouted, "Oh!" She proceeded to inhale the remainder of her food and run into the den. I stood and followed.

When I got into the room, I saw Annie staring at the chessboard. She moved a single piece and stared for a few more seconds before turning her gaze to meet mine.

Her smile nearly swallowed her face.

"Checkmate!"

- ◈ - **Chapter 8** - ◈ -

Edgar looked up from his writing, seven hours had passed since he started. Within the first one or two, his pencils had gone dull, and he switched to the pen, which had run out of ink fairly quickly. When he'd asked the guard that had taken over the shift after Roach left to sharpen his pencils, the guard refused and brought Edgar another of the flexible pens, a safer option. Edgar didn't mind randomly switching the medium to his salvation, but now the new pen was just about empty as well.

He wanted to continue but would need another pen. It was well into the night, and the guard had taken advantage of the quiet to catch a few zs of his own. Edgar refused to wake him. The guard shouldn't be sleeping on duty, but it was none of Edgar's concern. It occurred to Edgar, for the first time, that this particular guard fit the common stereotype of prison guards. He was a heavyset man, prone to propping up his legs and dozing off, earning him the nickname "Nyquil" among the other guards, and he, more often than not, had a box of donuts or pizza with him – this night it was donuts.

Not wanting to wake up Officer Nyquil, Edgar succumbed to his fatigue and, with a sore back and cramping hand, drifted off to sleep.

***

He turned the DVD over in his hands, inspecting it. "FOR EDDIE, WATCH ALONE," it was labeled. The DVD was left in Edgar's mailbox. There was no mystery of who had left it, Edgar recognized the handwriting, all capital letters, backward threes for the e's, and that it said *Eddie* rather than Edgar. It was Mike, Amy's new fiancé. Mike had never stopped calling Edgar Eddie, it was his way of belittling him. It had been Amy's idea for him to stop going by Eddie, but Edgar assumed it was brought about by something Mike had said before the affair began.

If Mike sent the DVD, then nothing good could come out of watching it; still, Edgar's curiosity got the better of him, and he slid the DVD into his computer. His computer prompted him to play the video, and Edgar hit the start button.

As the video began, all Edgar could see was a close up of Mike's face as he adjusted the camera. Mike stepped back from the camera and Edgar could see exactly what was being filmed.

Mike was in his bedroom; the camera faced the front of his bed. Amy was on the bed, adorned with a set of red lingerie so thin they were nearly transparent. With the camera set up, Mike crawled on next to her. Amy giggled, glancing at the camera briefly before returning her attention to Mike.

For the entirety of the hour and a half long video, Edgar sat transfixed, unable to pull his eyes away from the screen or to remove the disk. Dull pain in his chest troubled him throughout the viewing, accompanied by an increase in his heart-rate and shortness of breath. These symptoms increased in intensity when the recorded couple came to climax; Edgar almost lost consciousness from the increased blood pressure and decreased oxygen intake, but, now sharp, pain in his chest denied him that.

When the digital Mike stopped panting, he stood up and approached the camera. Mike adjusted the camera so that it showed both his face and the bed; Amy remained on the bed panting. Edgar had always been the last to stop panting, though most of the time he was the only one. The twisted smile on Mike's face told Edgar that at some point along the line, Amy had told him that little detail.

The picture rocked as Mike picked up the camera and walked over to Amy. She was on her back, her nude body glistened with sweat. She managed to catch her breath long enough to smile at the camera. Mike turned it back to himself; he wore another of his malicious smiles as he turned the camera off.

Coldness washed over Edgar, both slowing his heart and steadying his breathing. Edgar was filled with longing for his ex-wife. Despite the many years it'd been, Edgar thought Amy looked just as beautiful as when they first met. Edgar felt his body warm again. The image of Amy naked had aroused him. With that thought in mind, Edgar migrated to his room to pleasure himself.

Forty-five minutes, and three failed attempts, later, Edgar gave up and settled down for a restless night of sleep.

Each time Edgar came close to finishing, Mike's grinning visage appeared in his mind and stole his vigor, and so, Edgar went to bed unsatisfied.

***

After seven hours of lying in bed, Edgar had accumulated a total of two hours of sleep, he wandered back downstairs to the living room. After closing all of the blinds, he sat down on the chair in front of the television. He started Mike's video from the beginning. He fast-forwarded the tape until he came across a particular scene he vaguely remembered. In it, they were angled in such a way that almost all of Amy was visible, but only the top of Mike's head and shoulders were. They only remained like that for about three minutes, so Edgar had to rewind the footage twice before he managed to finish. Afterward, Edgar rewound the video to the beginning of the scene and paused it, before turning off the television and heading back to bed. He felt shameful, but he also felt satisfied enough to sleep.

Chapter 9

Edgar didn't wake up flustered or in pain like he usually did after an uncomfortable nightmare, he woke up grim and determined. The dream had been emotionally painful and upsetting, but Edgar used the pain to further steel his nerves. The memories of Mike and Amy weren't good ones by a long shot, but Edgar was able to use them to stoke his inner fires.

Edgar looked at the table; a solitary cookie remained. Throughout the previous evening, he'd eaten the rest of them while writing. He was long out of juice and with its chaser gone, the last cookie sat to die alone.

There was still an hour until breakfast and Edgar was, for the first time in a while, feeling famished. He didn't want to begin writing with his tank on empty, so Edgar decided to refresh himself. He'd felt reasonably pleasant after washing his hands and face the day before, so this morning he decided to take a shower.

It had been so long since Edgar's last shower that the water turned a brownish-gray as several layers of dirt and dead skin sloughed off, even several of his few remaining hairs decided to make a swim for freedom. Edgar envied them, not that they'd escaped the cell, but that they'd escaped him. Oh, how he wished he could once again escape himself, to mindlessly wander about his macabre shell for his last days.

He didn't linger on those thoughts, instead opting to return to those of his past to steel his nerve. As he stood in the shower, he cycled between picturing his latest nightmare and the next fragment of his story to ensure he stayed sufficiently motivated.

When Edgar stepped out of the shower, he noticed the breakfast tray had already been placed in his bean-hole. Had he really spent an hour in the shower? It didn't feel like an hour to him, but his sense of time was askew from months of timeless monotony.

Edgar saw the guard exiting but called for him. The guard considered Edgar with a perplexed expression. When Edgar requested a pen, the guard shrugged and said, "I'll see what I can find." Edgar supposed that was the best he'd get. He sat down and ingested greenish scrambled eggs, stale yet soggy toast, and a yellow-orange half they served him for breakfast. Forty-five minutes passed before the guard came back around to collect the dirty trays and, to Edgar's surprise, the guard dropped off a flex-pen as he did so.

With his nerves as steeled as they were going to get, Edgar began writing once more, hoping that he'd be able to maintain this foreign willpower through the more perilous depths of his mind.

***

One morning, no more than a month after Annie and Cynthia moved into the neighborhood, I received a phone call from my darling sister. "Hey, Eddie…err, Edgar!" she sounded excited. "I was unpacking my boxes, and I found one I hadn't unpacked since before I even got married. Do you remember back when we were kids, and I kept stealing your toys?" As I recalled, we were plenty older than kids the last time she stole from me, perhaps even early high school, though my memory was foggy. I told her I remembered, figuring the exact period was irrelevant.

"Well I stashed them all away in a box I kept in the back of my closet. I must have overlooked it every time I moved. I'm going to bring it by; could you meet me at your door, it's kind of heavy? I'm headed over now."

I hastened to the door, curious about the lost treasures of my youth, and opened it. I didn't immediately see Cynthia, and after five minutes of waiting, closed the door and sat down. Fifteen minutes later I heard my sister's footsteps approach. I opened the door with alacrity and ushered her in.

"I'm so sorry," she panted, "On my way out, Annie said she wanted a snack, so I got delayed. As soon as I finished, I ran all the way over."

"Oh, no worries," I said, "I'm sure kids are quite the hassle."

"You don't know the half of it," she chuckled. "Every other day it's food, food, food." We shared a brief laugh before Cynthia dropped the box on the coffee table. "I only glanced inside, I wanted to go through it with you. I know returning them now doesn't do much good, but at least we can look back together."

"That sounds nice," I said as Cynthia unfolded the flaps of the box. Inside, I saw an odd assortment of toys, trinkets, school supplies, and even some drawings.

"You know," Cynthia said softly, "I imagined myself a pirate, stealing booty and hiding it away. It's weird to look back and see just how cruel my games were. I hope I can make it up to you one day."

"There's no need," I reassured her. "We were kids, we're adults now, we know better."

Cynthia let her gaze drop to the floor. "The sad part is, I didn't realize it until well into my adult years, when I was with my ex-husband. That man was evil Edgar, there's no other word for it. The things he did…" She paused and wiped her eye, "Well, it really put things into perspective and made me reevaluate my life and childhood. I may not have been him, Edgar, but I was a real piece of shit."

We sat in silence for a moment, neither of us sure what to say. Cynthia continued looking down with vacant eyes. She was no longer in my house, she was somewhere in the past. Her eyes began to water, but no tears fell, at least, I didn't let them fall. I put my hand on her shoulder, stealing back her gaze, she was shocked at first, but her visage softened in my warm smile. "Let's see what's in here," I offered.

As we scoured the box, we unearthed various fragments of my childhood. Out of the box came my paddle-ball from age seven, my Pokémon cards from age 12, my colored pencils from age ten – as well as several illustrations of trees, cars, rivers, dogs, and clouds. There were even three of the journals I used as diaries and sketchbooks. A toy truck from age five, my running shoes from the same age, an autographed photo of my favorite middle school author, a plethora of fountain and ballpoint pens. We kept pulling more and more memories out of the box, half of the items I could remember the very day they went missing. A water-gun from age 11, a baseball from age nine.

We both paused when she withdrew a faded blue dog leash. Her eyes went wide, and my chest curled itself in knots, all but halting my breathing.

"I'm sorry," Cynthia whispered as much as cried. "I know I said that wine was for celebrating, but I really need a drink right now." With that, she dashed to the kitchen. I could hear her rummage through the cabinets and pull out a glass, dropping another in the process, it shattered across the floor. My breathing quickly became ragged as an asthma attack took me. My ears filled with a high pitch whistle and my vision blurred.

I lose track of time during the episodes I lose vision. It didn't make much sense for asthma since I shouldn't lose sight until my brain is severely deprived of oxygen, but in these episodes, my vision fled too quickly for it to be that. I worried about them and saw a doctor, but she referred me to a psychiatrist saying that my episodes were likely Post Traumatic Stress Disorder. I was too scared of an official diagnosis and never scheduled an appointment.

Eventually, the whistle faded just before my breathing returned, and my vision normalized last. With my senses under my control again, I staggered into the kitchen. I was greeted by the sight of Cynthia drawing deeply from a glass of wine. Judging by the level of the bottle, it was at least her third glass. She lifted her head and met my eyes momentarily before dropping them back to her drink. "He used to beat me you know," she said in a hushed tone. "Dad. He used to beat me. Not like a parent disciplining a child, he actually beat me. I think that's why I was such a troubled child. That's why I always picked on you. That's why—" she swallowed, "That why I killed Tomo. I know that doesn't excuse my actions or make it any better, but I just want you to understand. I wasn't angry at you or the puppy, I was angry at Dad, and you and Tomo suffered for it. Afterward, I blamed the whole thing on Dad, even your injuries. That's where the whole ordeal with Mom and Dad really began, they may have started fighting a few months before then, but that really kicked it off. My injuries were never visible, but yours that day… I'm sorry. I'm so sorry, Edgar."

I embraced her as she started sobbing. "I forgive you, Cynthia. It's okay."

"It's not okay!" she countered. "Because of me, Tomo died! Because of me, you got hurt! Because of me, you, to this day, have a breathing problem! That day, I ruined your life, and you think it's okay?!"

"No one person is at fault," I said, trying to calm my hysterical sister. "But you know what? The past is the past, let's exorcise those ghosts and spend our efforts making the future better."

"But Edgar, you don't understand. I know Dad wasn't a saint, but that's what initially drove the wedge between him and Mom, which lead to their divorce; and you know how he reacted to that. Edgar, in a roundabout way, I'm responsible for Dad's suicide!"

When I viewed it in that light, I could see why she'd think she was responsible, but it was still irrational.

"Cynthia, Mom would have left Dad eventually when she learned he was abusing you. What you did may not have been the honest thing to do, but it did manage to stop him from hurting you." She seemed to relax a bit at that, but a cloud passed over her face.

"You're right, Edgar, it did stop the abuse, eventually. But between that day and the day he got arrested, the abuse worsened, Edgar, you can't imagine how bad it got."

I hadn't known that our father had gotten arrested, but it made sense considering the situation, at the time I was young and distracted by Tomo's death and Cynthia's bullying. It would make sense they wouldn't clue me in on all the details at that age.

"Don't worry, Cynthia," I started, "I'm here for you if you need to talk."

She smiled and shook her head, no. "Maybe one day, Eddie, but I think I've unloaded enough of my burdens on you." We left it at that and cleaned up the shards of glass. She thanked me once more and departed. I sat in the living-room and inspected the contents of the box more thoroughly. I picked up the leash and turned it over in my hands, for the most part, it looked to be in the same condition it was all those years ago. Ragged from being gnawed on and stretched. The only difference was the accumulation of dust and a slight fading of the color. I cleaned it off and put it to the side. I planned to put everything else back in the box and store it in a closet or something, but I needed to find the leash in its own home.

As I continued to dig through the box, something caught my eye. One of the three journals wasn't mine. They were all the same type of journal, the black and white composition notebooks you could get two for a dollar at Walmart, but one of them had a few of the pages folder over at the corner, a little impromptu bookmark that was a pet peeve of mine and one of the reasons I don't pick up books from the library, despite that being the cheaper route considering how many books I read for my job. Curious as to the origins of this mystery journal, I opened it to a random page and read a few lines.

"...so, I went and peeked into the door, I didn't know what they were doing, but they were naked and were really loud (they must have thought I was still at Jenny's house)."

It looked like Cynthia's handwriting, but I couldn't guess how old, perhaps some time in late elementary school or early middle school based on the grammar and misspelled words. I can't remember the exact errors, but I probably would have still corrected them if I had. My first thought after reading those lines was that Cynthia had stumbled upon our parents making love while they thought she was out. Intrigued, I kept reading.

"... It was gross, they were inside each other. I wanted to run or scream or something, but I couldn't move. Daddy never noticed me (he was looking up), but the woman did."

"The woman?" I thought out loud.

"...she was sitting up and saw me. First, she looked scared, but then she smiled, and we looked in each other's eyes. Then I ran, but Daddy never knew I was there..."

I closed the journal. I don't know why, but it felt wrong. I was somehow intruding on not just adolescent Cynthia's privacy, but also my deceased father. I was learning too much about my old man. I thought he was just a man with a failed marriage who got depressed enough to take his own life. All this talk of abuse and information about an affair was hard to swallow. So many aspects of my childhood began making sense, and it astounded me that I hadn't been the least bit curious about it before now.

I put the journal back in the box. I'd have to return this to Cynthia, I had no right to read it, although I suspected I would feel differently had those first few lines been something more akin to, *"Dear diary, Jenny is such a bitch!"* Something you'd expect a grumpy little girl to write, not necessarily sunshine and rainbows, but ultimately just as innocent. This was too much for me to handle.

I didn't bother to go through the rest of the box, between the leash and Cynthia's diary, I was disheartened. I even placed the leash back in before putting the box in the closet of one of my spare bedrooms.

With a cup of coffee and a book in hand, it took me no time at all to forget about the box and its unsettling contents.

***

A few days later, another oddity occurred. It was a Wednesday morning, I was enjoying a cup of coffee and a book, the coffee more so than the book, when the doorbell rang. I paused to consider who it might be. Cynthia? She usually called first. Salesman? I hope not, I was short on funds. Mormon? I wish they could give me faith. I sat a moment too long, and the doorbell rang three more times in rapid succession. The latter two options wouldn't ring the bell so rapidly, so it had to be somebody I knew. Maybe some kids playing a prank? When I answered the door, I saw Annie standing there.

I looked around, expecting to see Cynthia walking up, but saw nobody. "Is something wrong?" I asked.

"No," she said, hands behind her back with a mischievous smile on her face.

"Then why are you here?"

"I wanted to come over and play."

"Oh, well, come in, I guess. I wasn't expecting company." She scampered in and dropped her turtle backpack in the middle of the floor. She opened it and rifled through it, placing its contents on the floor. I stole a glance at the clock, a quarter past nine.

"Shouldn't you be in school?" I asked.

"No school today," she said, not looking up. "Teacher workday."

"Okay, did your mother decide you were old enough to walk yourself over?"

"Mom doesn't know there's no school today." She looked up from the bag and met my eyes with those emerald orbs, "Please don't tell her!"

"Don't worry, I won't." As I said the words, she visibly relaxed and continued gutting the turtle.

"Aha!" she cheered, pulling a small figurine out of the bag. It was a bipedal turtle wearing a mask and holding nunchucks. "I found him on the playground today, I think he'll fit on the board. Can we replace one of the pieces with him?"

"Sure," I said. "Is that why you wanted to come over?"

"Yeah, I mean, Mom's not home, and I don't have school, so it's basically Saturday, which means I should be here." She gave a big toothy smile looking proud at her own cleverness.

"… Well," I said after a pause, "I guess you want to play chess now? Or did you want a snack first?"

"Snack first!" she said, stuffing the contents of her backpack back inside it.

"Okay, well since I wasn't expecting you, you'll have to wait for me to cook a batch of cookies. I hope that's okay."

"Don't worry, Uncle Ed, I'll survive."

While I went about the task of making cookies, Annie sipped on juice and sat at the chessboard, trying to determine which piece she'd replace with the turtle. She eventually decided on the queen, which seemed odd since the turtle looked male to me, but I guess she wanted her strongest piece to possess nun-chucks and wandered into the kitchen to harass the cookies as they slowly roasted to death.

"Your patience for certain things always impresses me, Annie," I said. She looked away from the oven long enough to throw a smile in my direction before returning her attention back to the oven. "But, sometimes you're impatient." This time, the look she threw was one of confusion, and her attention didn't immediately return to the oven.

"When it comes to the stuff you like," I continued, "Your focus is absolute, like when we play games, or you're waiting for cookies, but when you're waiting to do something you like, going walking through the woods, for instance, you can't get there soon enough."

She cocked her head at me, staring at me as if I were a simpleton. "What do you mean?" she asked. "I'm not impatient when we're headed out for a hike."

"But you can't focus on anything else during that time," I countered.

"Exactly!" she said triumphantly as she turned around again.

"What?"

She sighed and turned back to me, "You're slow, Uncle Ed."

"I'm sorry, I just don't understand what you mean."

"Of course, I can't focus on anything else, all of my focus is used preparing for the hike. I'm not being impatient, I'm just ready." I couldn't refute the logic. It wasn't so much a lack of focus but just that it was directed elsewhere. I was about to express my understanding, but her attention had returned to the incubating cookies.

I suddenly realized I had forgotten to start the timer on the oven and was afraid the cookies would burn. I was about to open my mouth to say something, but Annie grabbed the oven mitts and extracted the cookie sheet. "How do you know they're done?" I asked, "There's no timer."

"I keep track of it in my head," she stated matter-of-factly. "You forget the timer a lot."

"But we talked for a bit, didn't you lose your place?"

"No, I keep it going in the background. It's pretty easy if I'm not doing anything complicated like chess."

I was impressed, Annie was a lot smarter than I gave her credit for. I didn't think she was dumb, in fact, I thought she was incredibly bright for her age, but this was, assuming her internal clock was accurate, genius level. I was storing the information away for later when I realized something. "You said I forget the time a lot?"

"Yep."

"And you watch the oven every time I forget to set the timer?"

"Yep."

I thought back to how often Annie watched the oven and felt embarrassed at the frequency.

***

During the next few weeks, Annie began showing up on random evenings after school. I didn't mind the company, it was refreshing to watch my niece eat cookies, play chess, and go on nature walks. We even watched movies on occasion. Every now and then she replaced another chess piece with a different figurine. Her knights were colorful plastic ponies, her king and queen were both turtles, and all of her pawns were replaced with acorns we glued onto tiny pieces of plywood to stop them from rolling off the board. The change in pieces threw me off, but after a while, I acclimated. Annie seemed to have no difficulty adapting to the changes. We continued to play and at least a couple of times each game I would inadvertently make a mistake so Annie could either win or come close; the more we played, the less deliberate errors I had to make. She learned quickly, but what impressed me most wasn't how fast she learned, but how well she learned.

One Saturday we were playing a game of chess, and she made a move that would cost her dearly, possibly the whole game – she made this mistake in the previous game too.

Since I was in the habit of avoiding huge leads, I didn't take the piece and instead put one of my own pieces in jeopardy.

Annie caught me off guard with her next move. Instead of taking my piece, she moved another valuable piece into peril – was she having an off day? I responded similarly.

"What are you doing?!" she demanded.

Shocked at the sudden outburst, all I could manage was, "What?"

"Why didn't you take either of my pieces? I practically gave them to you!"

"I didn't see the move, but now that you mention it, I do see a better move I could—"

"Don't lie to me, Mister!" She only called me mister when she was mad at me. "You saw it, and you saw it last game too! You've been going easy on me!"

Caught red-handed, I gave in. "Okay, it's true, I have been going easy on you. I just didn't want you to get discouraged."

"I can't believe it. Why do you think it's okay to go easy on me? Do you think I'm dumb?"

"No, I don't think you're dumb. In fact, I think you're quite brilliant."

"So, you sabotaged my training? Are you that much of a sore loser?"

"What?"

"You're training me wrong, and you're doing it on purpose! Is it so I won't be able to catch up or beat you?"

"Training?" I asked, "I thought we were just playing for fun, and I figured it wouldn't be fun to lose over and over."

"I would have won eventually, you didn't need to go easy."

"I'm sorry, Annie. You have gotten a lot better though."

"Not enough," she said, her eyes brimming with water. "If you do dumb things on purpose, it doesn't help. You were better than me, so I copied how you played. There was a tournament yesterday at school, I wanted to win and show you the trophy…" She paused and wiped her eyes before continuing, angry again. "But I lost! I copied the things you did, and it made me lose the last game!" She started crying.

"I'm so sorry, Annie," I said, wrapping her in a hug. "I didn't know you were taking chess so seriously."

"I take everything seriously!" she shot back between tears.

"Tell you what, Annie. I won't go easy on you ever again, and from now on, I'm going to make sure your *training* is top-notch."

***

After that day, I stopped going easy on Annie while playing chess. On occasion, when I legitimately made a bad move, she eyeballed me, trying to determine whether the move was intentional or not. I don't know how, but in those moments, her eyes seemed to grow several shades darker.

Annie started leaving early for the school bus so we could knock out a couple of rounds of speed chess. Within a couple of weeks, she managed to take a few games off of me every now and then, and when the school's monthly chess tournament came back around, she brought home first place in standard chess and third place in speed chess.

The following month, she took first in both.

***

Those few months I spent with Annie playing chess were some of the happiest of my life. I managed to stop thinking about my ex-wife and got back into the favorite pastime of my teen years. I was sleeping better and no longer needed the aid of pills. I still continued paying for and picking up my prescription because I didn't want to go through the process of canceling it – most of it would be automated with voice recordings, but in my experience, any attempted cancellation of services yielded an actual person joining the call to try and force a change of heart – so I ended up building a small stash in my medicine cabinet.

I wanted to have Annie enter some of the regional chess tournaments but knew that that level of competition would eat her alive. She was brilliant, but some of those kids practiced and trained with the Masters and Grandmasters of the sport; all Annie had was me. I did, however, manage to get my hands on several books written by those legendary players.

Ultimately though, the enjoyment wasn't about chess. Yes, I enjoyed playing, but I'm sure it could have been replaced with any number of other activities, even something as simple as the occasional walks, we took through the woods or the card games we played when we burned out on chess. I began to think of Annie as my own daughter. I went shopping with her, helped her study for school (an easy task considering her exceptional intelligence and seemingly flawless memory), and even played host to a slumber party or two. I was proud of my sister for raising such a respectful and intelligent daughter, despite the cruel husband.

With Annie, in my mind, at least, being like a daughter to me, it was natural that I would be concerned when I saw bruises on her arms. It wasn't anything serious looking. Every now and then I'd see a bruise on her forearm when she pulled back her sleeves to wash her hands (she had an affinity for long sleeves). Anytime I questioned her, she would say she fell or something while playing at school. I didn't doubt her answers, as children often hurt themselves playing, especially ones as energetic and tunnel-visioned as Annie, and I'd also never known Annie to lie to me.

There was a turning point, however, on the day we went swimming.

– ✪ – Chapter 10 – ✪ –

The lights went out, leaving Edgar in darkness and halting his progress of the next arc of his story. The storm had picked up over the last few hours, the incessant rain and wind had drowned out most of the noise save for the occasional deafening thunderclap. Lightning wasn't too distracting since the window in his cell was diminutive, but that last flash was close and not only blinded Edgar temporarily but took out the power to his block.

Within moments, the emergency lights flickered to life, but they were little more than a dim yellow bar of light located above his cell door. It permitted him only enough vision to move without fear of impacting furniture, not enough to write.

Edgar thought the storm had been nearing its conclusion earlier, when he had showered, he never would have believed it'd frenzy again. If it were going like this, Edgar would have skipped the shower; the thought struck Edgar as queer. He was going to die soon anyway, wanted to even, but he was afraid to risk being struck by lightning in the shower? Would he have cared a few days ago before he started writing? Edgar didn't have an absolute answer, but he figured that he wouldn't have cared. Then again, a few days ago, Edgar wouldn't have taken a shower, so the point was moot.

As the storm continued, it increased its intensity, rattling the walls with each concussive burst of thunder. No matter how close the lightning came or how fast the wind blew, the facility held strong. It occurred to Edgar that the safest place to be during a storm was probably prison. It just wouldn't do if some natural disaster came in and freed all of the prisoners, the public would panic, and the local communities would surely find themselves in more danger once the peril of the storm passed. Edgar tried to picture the relief effort coming in, only to be delayed or scared off by fleeing convicts seeking sanctuary.

Edgar continued distracting his thoughts while he waited for the power to return. After half an hour, Edgar grew impatient and crawled into his bunk to sleep instead. The occasional peal of thunder accentuated the cacophony of the storm and startled him awake, despite that, Edgar managed to doze.

***

Eddie lay on the bed attempting to sleep. Loud crashes and bangs accompanied the shouts and curses of the argument his parents were sharing. Eddie didn't know what was happening. His parents had gotten along well until just recently. Now all they did was argue. They really increased the intensity two weeks ago, when Tomo died. Eddie's superficial injuries had healed, but his broken ribs left him with a wheeze.

Eddie hadn't done much since Tomo died. What confused Eddie was that neither of his parents asked him how he acquired his injuries. His mom just silently took him to the hospital when she got home that evening. Initially, he hid in his room, sad and ashamed, but his mother found her way upstairs and, without a word, escorted him out.

The doctor took some X-rays, cleaned some cuts and scrapes, and given Eddie some mild painkillers for the breaks, they were weak, but anything stronger would have been unhealthy for a child his age. His physical injuries, coupled with the psychological trauma, left Eddie in a daze for over a week. During that time, Eddie barely saw his father. In one particular argument between his folks early on, Eddie heard his mother demand, "If you weren't in the forest, then where were you?!"

Eddie's father paused, then stumbled over a few words, but ultimately, he didn't have an answer for her.

"What? No alibi?" she continued, growing more heated. Eddie peeked down the stairs to watch his parents in secret. His mother's face was burning red, and his father's was pale and sweaty. "I can't believe you would do this!"

"I already told you I didn't!" his father countered, getting rustled himself, his face beginning the transition from white to red.

"Then where were you?!"

Eddie's father opened his mouth to answer, shut it, and turned beet red. He spun in frustration, swinging his arms wide. The maneuver knocked a nearby vase off of its pedestal, bringing it crashing down to the floor, scattering shards of ceramic and ash.

Eddie's father spun back in surprise just as Eddie's mother lunged forward in a motion to catch the already fallen vase; the back of his hand came slapping across the side of her face. Eddie's mom reeled in shock, holding the side of her face, his dad froze in terror at the unexpected contact.

"How dare you," she said, nearly silent. Eddie's father remained frozen. "How dare you!" she shrieked in outrage.

"You know that wasn't my intention," his father said, his hands up. "I didn't know you were jumping forward."

"You just so happen to conveniently backhand me across the face as I'm yelling at you. I'm sure the whole thing was an accident, wasn't it? The woods, the dog, the vase, the slap! How convenient none of it was your fault, it was all a damn accident! Well, now I can rest easy!"

"I would never do any of that."

"You just did!"

Eddie's father stumbled over a few more words but again didn't manage to finish any of them. Frustrated, he threw his hands down and fled the room. Eddie likewise fled the top of the stairs. After moving the first few feet silently, he ran to his room and sat on his bed, digesting what he just saw.

A few minutes later Eddie's mother stalked into his room. "How are you feeling sweetie?" she asked, sitting down adjacent to him on the bed.

"I'm okay," Eddie wheezed.

"Still having a hard time breathing, huh?" Eddie nodded. Eddie's mom opened her mouth to say something but closed it after a brief pause. She looked like she wanted to ask him a question but thought better of it. She stared blankly, thoughts flitting across her face. At one point her hand rose unconsciously to the side of her face. After a few more moments, she kissed him on the forehead and left. He heard her enter Cynthia's room and start a conversation with her. Eddie didn't bother eavesdropping. He didn't want to listen to that conversation. Eddie just stretched out and went to sleep.

***

Now, more than three weeks after the incident in the woods, his parents were arguing again, as was the daily norm now. A particularly loud crash startled Eddie, and he bolted upright, sending a jolt of pain through his chest. His mother was screaming. She had been mad when the vase had broken, now she was in a rage. Her voice was more feral screech than an angry shout. His dad was yelling too, an angry, yet defensive, roar.

His mother's shrieks were on occasion accompanied by a crash, bang, or thud as she threw something. His father's shouts would stop momentarily just before each crash and would increase in intensity for a few seconds after each one, as if to make up for the lost time.

Eddie wanted to eavesdrop but thought better of the idea, some of the words were loud enough or repeated often enough, for him to hear anyways. "How could you?!" and "Get out you, bastard!" from his mother and, "How could you think that?!" and "You, crazy bitch!" from his father.

The encounter went on for several minutes, Eddie didn't know there were so many throw-able objects downstairs. At one point, Eddie thought it was over, but his mom had made her way to the kitchen and started throwing silverware, pots, pans, and other various cooking utensils. It was one of these crashes that had startled Eddie upright. Eddie was surprised that during the entirety of her tantrum, not once did he hear something resound with the thick, moist impact of hitting flesh. Maybe his mother wasn't aiming for his dad, or maybe his father was nimbler than he looked.

Eventually, the banging stopped, but their voices continued battling for several more minutes. Eddie missed the final points of the argument as their voices fluctuated and were only loud enough to be understood if they were throwing insults. Near the end, Eddie finally heard something with more context than, "bastard," "little bitch," and "liar." His mother had begun yelling, "I'm calling the police!"

And his father picked up the cries of, "You're crazy," "Go ahead," and "I don't give a fuck!" His father must have been bluffing though, because he eventually left, slamming the door on his way out.

Eddie wanted to run after his father and apologize, to tell him it wasn't his fault Tomo died, that all fault lied with him and that Mom was mad at the wrong person, but Eddie was too scared. If Eddie had known that that would be his last chance to see his father, he would have braved it.

– ⊛ – Chapter 11 – ⊛ –

Edgar woke to the rebirth of his lights. Shortly after, a guard came and verified Edgar's identity, as was protocol after a power outage. The pile of papers on his table reminded Edgar of the task at hand. He needed to finish writing about his trip to the pool with Annie. He looked at the pages and was disheartened to see how little of that part he managed to write.

He stared out his window, the storm had played out its fury, but a heavy rain persisted. Edgar sighed, he'd been motivated before, now it all felt like a chore. Was it the weather? Or was it just the natural reaction now that the happiest memories had passed. There were good times past this point, but they were all sprinkled with pain, stress, and worry.

He grabbed a pen and his stack of papers. With a sigh, he continued writing.

***

It was a Friday that began like any other. I went about my usual tasks, reading, drinking coffee, and stocking up on cookies and juice for the weekend. Annie arrived at my door as soon as the bus delivered her from school. Cynthia had ceased escorting her within the first month. The only difference this Friday was that Annie arrived bearing a DVD.

"I borrowed a movie from my teacher, Uncle Ed. Can we watch it?"

"I don't see why not," I responded. "What's it about?"

"It's about the ocean. We were watching it in class because we had a substitute, but we didn't get to finish. There were sharks and dolphins and stuff. There were turtles too, but that was the part we stopped at. That's why I had to borrow it."

***

Something donned on me. "How did you borrow it from your teacher if she was absent?"

"I just borrowed it." I nodded as if in understanding, I didn't bother explaining to her that you needed permission to borrow things and that even if you intend to return it, that it still counted as stealing. It didn't seem to matter now anyway since she already had the DVD in her possession.

"Well then, let's grab some snacks and watch it."

The movie turned out to be a three-hour documentary about ocean wildlife and, despite my suggestion that we start the film where she left off, she insisted we start at the beginning. That meant we spent an extra 45 minutes on the couch. I didn't mind a great deal, I wasn't a big fan of ocean fauna, but I did happen to find documentaries delightful. The video covered a broad range of ocean dwellers, including several I hadn't known existed. Annie came out of it with a newfound love of octopus and a heightened interest in turtles.

Another oddity that came out of Annie watching the documentary was the sudden desire to go swimming. It was still relatively early in the evening, her school let out around two-thirty, so despite watching the three-hour film, we still had two or three hours of daylight left.

"Swimming?" I asked. "Do you even know how to swim?"

"Of course!" she stated with pride. "My dad taught me when I was little…" She paused. "Littler."

"Hmm," I said. "I suppose that saves me the trouble of teaching you. I'd be terrible at it anyway."

"You taught me how to play chess," she countered.

"That was your own genius, not my crummy teaching."

She beamed at the compliment. "So that means we're going swimming, right?"

"Sure, why not," I said. "Did you pack a swimsuit?"

"No."

"Do you need to grab one from your house?"

"I don't have one," she said, eyes growing wide like a puppy.

I smirked, realizing that Annie did take after my sister a little. "Well then, I guess we'll have to go shopping first."

She beamed again and hopped to her feet, "Let's hurry then, or there won't be much time to swim!"

When we arrived at the store, I expected us to spend too long shopping to actually swim, but we managed to get in and out in under 15 minutes. Annie picked the style of swimsuit, and I chose the color, green to match her eyes.

We embarked on our journey to the pool; the neighborhood we resided in provided and maintained one at the corner of the block. There were bathrooms, showers, and even a party house available for rent. Since there were locations to change at, we didn't bother stopping on the way there from the store to avoid wasting any more daylight.

When we arrived, I had barely managed to park the car before Annie leaped out of it. She was held up at the gate and had to wait for me to catch up with the key – all residents were given a key, and I kept it on my key-chain despite never having had any intent to use it. Once granted entry, she bolted for the changing room. I meandered my way to one, not in any particular hurry to change into my own swimsuit. The changing rooms were little more than concrete stables with benches. Derelict remains of old pool toys decorated the floor, and somehow the chlorine smell that accompanied pools was more intense inside, it felt almost palpable. The floor was wet in many places, and a fetid puddle sat in the center where the sole drain was clogged. It wasn't a particularly hot day, but the room was humid and uncomfortable. I started to change, wanting nothing more than to be out of there, but was stalled by the tightening of my chest. These particular assaults upon my respiratory system weren't nearly as common as they used to be, but they were also triggered by various environmental queues rather than just stress or excessive cardio. I'd been relatively free of them since meeting Annie, save for a few that accompanied our hikes when we traversed moderately difficult terrain.

I was forced to sit as a wave of nausea struck me. The bench was soggy, but at that moment I didn't care, all of my focus was on the breathing exercises my physician had suggested. I always managed to lose track of time during those episodes, sometimes they lasted a couple of minutes and sometimes upwards of 30. They all felt both instantaneous and endless. When I finally recovered my wits, I looked up and saw a man wearing a concerned expression staring back at me.

"Sir, are you okay?" he asked.

"Yes," I croaked, not being entirely honest but I knew that the sight of a wheezing, unresponsive man clenching his chest usually made bystanders assume the worst.

"You sure?" he persisted. "You're really pale and sweaty."

"I'll be fine," I said with more control. "This happens on occasion, it's a breathing issue, not a heart one."

"Well, that's good to hear I suppose," the man said, "at first I came to beat your ass, my son came in to change but came back out saying some dude was masturbating." I paused, confused, it was at that moment I realized the stage of dressing I stopped at. My pants and underwear were around my ankles, my trunks slung over my shoulder. My face went from white to red in an instant as I jumped up and returned my pants to my waist. The man laughed, "Given the situation, I can see my son's mistake. Walks in to see a man with his pants down breathing heavily and sitting in the corner." The man laughed again and left.

After spending a couple more minutes to catch my breath, I dropped my pants again, and this time, I managed to finish changing. When I emerged from my dank cave, the natural light of day, though the sun was on the retreat, stunned me. I stood transfixed for a few moments and adjusted. The smell was still that of chlorine, but unlike the stagnant air of the changing room, I found this air refreshing. The feeling didn't stick though; as I scanned the other swimmers, I noticed something was amiss.

Several people were stealing glances or staring, in one particular direction, many of them whispered to others. They wore either masks of concern or disgust. When I managed to ascertain the source of their attention, I too was gawking. I followed their gazes over to the end of the pool where Annie stood on the diving board. She stood erect, hands over her head in preparation to jump. Her hair was already soaked and clung to her back, the water made the orange look darker but gave it more shine. Her green one-piece swimsuit was likewise wet and sparkled in the sunlight. The illumination made all the colors of her person pop and glow. Most notable of which, were the purples and yellows that spotted her arms and legs.

The bruises on her upper arms were a series of small bruises next to each other as if she had been roughly grabbed. Larger bruises coated her lower shoulders, calves, and thighs as if she'd been struck. The bruises were in various cycles of their lives, most yellowed and nearly healed, though there were plenty of ripe purples stains and even a few locations where they overlapped. Annie was being continuously abused.

Her muscles flexed as she hopped twice before diving into the water. I caught part of the nearby conversation between a young olive-colored teenager, and a large darker woman I assumed was his mother. The teen was whispering and concealed his words well enough to prevent my hearing of them, but his mother shared none of his discretion. "Who did she come here with? Him?" She pointed at me, I pretended not to notice them. "Well, how else was I supposed to clarify? Wait, what? He was doing what in the changing room? Should… Should we call the police?"

I walked away before I could hear any more. Annie was climbing a ladder out of the pool, I approached her. "Let's go, Annie. There's something important I forgot to do this evening." She didn't question me or complain about leaving early, she just followed silently.

As I escorted Annie out of the pool, I tried to keep my eyes forward, but against my better judgment, they wandered. There were eight people at the pool, and every single set of eyes followed us out, their gazes filled with overt hate and contempt. I looked only for a moment, but to this day, I remember every single face from that scene. The darker woman with a loud voice and her mixed heritage son, perhaps 14 or so years old. The Caucasian man I talked to in the changing room, who I presumed was the teen's father, was across the pool. A pair of blonde girls, probably in their last year of high school or first year of college, with bronze tanned skin. A petite Hispanic woman with long dark hair sitting alone in the Jacuzzi. And a pair of pale elderly women made paler by the amount of sunscreen smeared on their faces. All of them watched us depart. None of them spoke to us as we did. Despite not being the one to put the bruises on Annie, those stares filled me with enough shame and guilt to make me feel as if I did. The whispered word *monster* followed me out.

Not a single word crossed between Annie and me on the ride back, I was grateful for it, I didn't know if I could hold a conversation with her at that moment without a respiratory malfunction or a breakdown into tears.

Initially, I thought Annie was ignorant of what had transpired at the pool and that she just read my emotions and decided it best not to speak. As I look back on it now, I believe she wasn't. Not only did she not talk about that evening again, but despite her appearing to have had an enjoyable time swimming, she never asked to return.

Nobody from the pool ever ended up reporting Annie's bruises to the authorities, or if they did nothing became of it. At the time I thought we were fortunate, now I realize that if something did become of it, we both would have been spared a great deal of pain. From that day on, there were no more carefree days with Annie. We would go on playing chess and going on hikes, but when looked at her, I saw a frightened child, suppressing the abuse she suffered and clinging to her uncle so that she may have some semblance of a proper parental figure. A pained frown lurked beneath each of her smiles.

Annie was a brilliant child, I can't believe she would take the care to hide her bruises from me all these months just to forget about them when she wanted to swim. It seems obvious now, but at the time I was blind. What might have been prevented if I had answered her subtle cries for help?

***

Over the next couple of weeks, I added a step to my morning and evening routine. I sat in my living room and watched Annie wait for the bus and watched as it dropped her off. Seeing Annie's bruises unsettled me and I had to see

105

if I could help her. The first issue was finding out where the bruises were coming from. It was apparent they weren't self-inflicted, so I assumed Annie had a school bully, the other option was to label Cynthia as the culprit, but I couldn't bring myself to believe it. The thought of my sister, who just wanted to better herself, right her wrongs, and take care of her only child, hurting Annie disgusted me. She still wasn't a model citizen, she drank on occasion, usually more than she should, and was too busy to always be there for Annie, but she was a single mother that had to work for a living. She can't be at two places at once or drop her only source of income, so it was acceptable, especially since I was more than willing to help them out.

While the angle of the bruises on her upper arms suggested they were inflicted by an adult, Annie was shorter than the majority of kids her age, so an exceptionally tall classmate, or older student, could have left such bruises on her. It was a more comforting thought than the alternative. I watched Annie get on and off the bus those two weeks, hoping I'd catch a glimpse of some schoolyard bully assaulting Annie – an odd thing to hope for in hindsight.

I didn't see anything while she waited for, or exited, the bus, and the brief glimpses I could get of her on the bus yielded the same results. I grew restless. I didn't want to believe Cynthia would treat her only daughter as she did me in our youth, I couldn't believe it; Annie was too open and friendly. If she really was suffering at the hands of her mother, would she not be as reserved and broken as I was? I couldn't very well follow her to school or watch her on the playground, so I settled on inspected her bruises from afar and keeping an eye out for any new discoloration. This made finding any evidence near impossible because of Annie's propensity to wear long-sleeved shirts or jackets. I had to use other factors to judge the situation. Did to seem afraid or anxious on her way to school? Did she perk up after leaving? I saw nothing in the following weeks to soothe my anxiety. She almost always seemed excited on her way to school, quietly awaiting the bus's arrival alone, kicking around some rocks or fiddling with one thing or another, and smiling as the bus drew near. More troubling were her expressions on those occasions I could spot her while riding the bus home, though more often than not I couldn't. She smiled and chatted with the other kids, but after waving them and bus bye, her face would darken as she walked home. Very telling, yes, but it's odd how good we are at believing comforting lies, especially those we tell ourselves.

Granted, I still lacked real evidence, Annie's change of emotions could be explained by any other number of things. She could very well just be dreading chores or homework as she left the bus and being bullied midday rather than on the bus. I was not only jumping to conclusions but dwelling on and dreading said conclusions. I also didn't have a plan one way or the other, school bully or abusive mother. By the time I made a plan, I had, despite my self-deception, come to believe Cynthia was the culprit.

It would have been an ingenious plan had anyone else carried it out; unfortunately, the only person I had at my disposal was myself. While at this point, I believed Cynthia was leaving bruises on Annie, I still held out more than a little hope that Annie was just the victim of some other child's issues.

The plan was a simple one, approach Cynthia, inform her Annie had bruises and that I was concerned about her having a bully. In the event Annie had a bully, Cynthia could contact the school and resolve the matter. I thought about trying it myself, but I couldn't bring myself to contact the school; at the time I wrote it off as something I shouldn't do since I wasn't her legal guardian and, other than the bruises themselves, there was no evidence. There was also the chance Cynthia would get in trouble if it turned out there wasn't a bully, I didn't want to put Annie or Cynthia through that ordeal at the time; besides, perhaps I could stop Cynthia if that was the case. Thoughts of orphanages and foster homes crossed my mind, further turning me away from the obvious best plan. The second part of my brilliant plan was that, in the event, Cynthia was responsible for the bruises, the suggestion of a school bully would let her know that others, or at the very least, I, were taking note of the abuse and she would have to lay off or stop entirely. It was subliminal intimidation under the guise of a concerned relative. It might have worked too if I were a more confident and forward individual, though it does occur to me that a more confident and forward person would likely have just informed the school or the proper authorities.

Just as a concerned neighbor from the pool could have stopped the suffering to come, this was a chance for me to do the same, but my lack of courage would not only ignore this one but every chance to come after it.

The day came when I would put my plan into action, but I got cold feet last minute and stayed home reading instead. I couldn't even bring myself to execute such a non-confrontational and straightforward plan. I managed to convince myself it was a fluke and that the bruises would stop appearing. More and more frequently, I would request Annie's aid in something that required her to roll up her sleeves, such as washing dishes, so that I could stay updated. To my dismay, not only did the bruises keep appearing, but they did so with increasing frequency. Still, another three weeks passed before I grew a pair and went to confront my sister.

When I finally decided to confront Cynthia, if you can call it a confrontation, it was five in the evening, and I was well into my eighth cup of coffee since noon. I was tense, jittery, and concerned about Annie. It wasn't out of the ordinary for Annie to stay home some evenings, but I was particularly anxious that day. The review I left for the young author whose works I had been sampling, but not particularly enjoying, had caused an outrage. Apparently, readers disagreed with my description of his work being overly dramatic and difficult for the casual reader to follow. It's an odd business where my honest and analytical reviews of literature were, in and of themselves, subject to the review of the masses. I attempted to defend my review, stating something along the lines of needing to be a scientist, philosopher, or a conspiracy theorist to fully appreciate his work and that while his writing was sound on a technical level, it wouldn't appeal to the average reader. The frequenters of my sight disagreed, many going so far as to unsubscribe for the review – nearly 15 percent of them! It would be detrimental to my financial stability if I didn't issue an apology and offer up a new, more positive, review, and cite some personal bias as the reason for my initial one.

Needless to say, I was unsettled and was hoping Annie would stop by and distract me from my site with a few rounds of chess. When she didn't arrive, I didn't worry, as I said, it wasn't out of the ordinary for Annie to stay home in the evenings, but it did shift the focus of my frustrations from work to Annie. The anonymous will of the internet was pushing me around, so perhaps it was time to push back, in person at least. Besides, my plan would mean there wouldn't be conflict, I'd designed it to negate such a thing. Just tell Cynthia that I believe Annie has a bully and the rest would work itself out.

Hyped up on caffeine and concern, I found myself knocking on Cynthia's door. During the brief walk over, I even managed to convince myself that it was indeed a school bully and made myself feel ridiculous and ashamed for not telling Cynthia sooner, what a terrible brother and uncle I was.

After knocking, but before receiving a response, it occurred to me that this was the first time I had visited Cynthia's house. It seemed queer to think that in the months she'd lived here, all of our conversations had either been over the phone or at my house. When she answered the door, I was caught off-guard by what was inside. The first thing I noticed was the mess, beer bottles and dirty laundry littered the floor, with dirt and dust clinging to every surface. The smell hit me a moment later, a heavy aroma of cigarette ash and smoke, accented by the sour-smelling mildew from old beer bottles.

I knew immediately that my reasoning of Annie having a bully was a farce; there was no doubt in my mind that it was Cynthia hurting Annie. The strength I'd accumulated from my frustration fled me, I wanted nothing more at that moment than to flee myself, to scurry away back to the sanctuary of my house. I was in the process of finding some way to explain my presence and excuse myself but was interrupted.

"What do you want?" Cynthia demanded, her words slurred.

I had a moment of panic as I fumbled for an excuse, but I came up short, and unwillingly continued with my original plan. I told her my theory about the bully and mentioned the bruises I saw on Annie when we went swimming. Cynthia, appearing unconcerned, called out for Annie, who appeared moments later, wearing a sleeveless shirt and a skirt, her bruises out for the world to see. She hadn't been hiding them from her mother. Cynthia knew about them, meaning my whole plan was doomed, she wouldn't be intimidated by my petty attempt at subtlety; she was parading Annie's bruises in front of me by calling her over.

"Yes, Ma'am?" Annie replied, eyes glued to her feet.

"Your uncle here has expressed concern about you having a bully at school. He said he saw your bruises when the two of you went swimming. Is this true?"

"No, Ma'am," she said, clasping her hands together.

"So, you didn't go swimming? Are you calling Uncle Edgar a liar?"

"No," Annie whispered as she wrung her fingers together.

"So, you did go swimming?" Cynthia reasoned.

"Yes," Annie squeaked.

"What have I told you about going swimming? It's too risky, you could drown."

"I'm sorry…" Annie was nearly crying.

"Very well, we'll discuss this in a minute, about the other issue, do you have a bully?"

"No, Ma'am."

"Then where did you get the bruises Uncle Edgar saw?"

"I fell down while playing tag," Annie said too quickly for it to have been a natural response.

"You're not lying to me, are you?"

"No, Ma'am. Never." Annie was too scared to notice her last response was a blatant lie since she had just confessed to lying about swimming; fortunately, Cynthia was too distracted, or too drunk, to notice.

"Very well, run along now," Cynthia said, and with that, Annie was off, offering me only the briefest of glances, her eyes pleaded for help, and, like the cowardly monster I am, I did nothing. Again.

Throughout the entire exchange between Annie and Cynthia, I stood frozen, the only movement my eyes darting from mother to daughter as they spoke. Aside from the portion about swimming, it all felt rehearsed and considering that Cynthia could clearly see Annie's bruises, unnecessarily so. The conversation played out as if Cynthia couldn't see Annie's injuries. If it was meant to be a cover story, the delivery alone attested to its falsehood, let alone the flawed logic of Annie getting bruises on the insides of her arms from falling down. Cynthia was far too clever and intelligent to think that anybody, even me, would buy that. Then again, she didn't need me to buy it, she knew what my reaction would be; I'd been a pushover and avoided conflict since my youth. Still, it almost seemed as if she wanted me to know it was a lie. She could have avoided any suspicion by blowing it off as a bully or just not calling Annie forward. She was testing me.

What would I do if I knew? Would I call her out? Would I report her? Or would I just fall in line like I always did? It wasn't much of a test, she knew the answer, and I knew she was testing me. The fact that I could see that and still remain passive was almost as infuriating as the truth of the matter itself.

"Well, that settles that," Cynthia said, pulling me from my thoughts.

"Right," I said unsteadily. "It's good to hear Annie doesn't have a bully."

"Yes, she just needs to be more careful," Cynthia added and disappeared back inside her house, leaving me standing there staring at the door.

*****

It was a week before I saw Annie again. I kept my habit of watching her bus, but Annie didn't get on or off of it. Come Friday, Annie appeared at my door to stay the weekend as usual. When she stepped inside, I realized why she hadn't been at school. The left side of her face showed a half-healed yellow and purple bruise, perhaps a week old.

Once the door closed, Annie wandered off. I froze. Seeing the results of my cowardice stole from me the luxury of movement. When I finally recovered my senses, I found Annie at the table drinking pineapple juice and waiting in front of the oven for a batch of coconuts cookies, as if nothing were amiss.

"I… I'm sorry," I stammered, unable to say anything else.

Annie looked at me, bewilderment plain on her face. "Don't apologize, you didn't know Mommy told me not to go swimming." Annie's sincerity shocked me, she could forgive me after I caused her so much pain, even go so far as to deny that it was me that caused it. I wrapped her in a strong hug, she flinched at first but returned the embrace once her initial surprise subsided.

Sharp hailstones of guilt began buffeting my soul. Annie either didn't understand my weakness in not seeking aid to stop her abuse, or she didn't care. That night, my internal hurricane blew back in with an intensity to make up for the lost time.

***

Edgar was unsure of the exact time of day it was or how long he'd been writing. The sky remained overcast with dark clouds, but the rain had stopped falling. Writing about his failings had been more taxing than he imagined. He hadn't had a full-on asthma attack, but his breathing had been shallow the past couple of hours. He stopped writing because it became physically difficult. The stress and regret accumulated and weighed him down.

He forced himself to breathe deeply and found some of his burden lifted, but he was still exhausted, and the grayness outside did little to lift his spirits. He decided now was as good a time as any to call it quits for the night. If these memories burdened him, the next set would surely over-encumber him if he wasn't fully rested. He set his pen down and put the notebook to the side.

Edgar couldn't believe how tired he could be from something as simple as writing. He crawled onto his mat to lose consciousness and bathed in his anxiousness about the next day's writing, unsure if he even had the strength, or the stomach, to continue. He put those thoughts away for later, closed his eyes, and let the nightmares take him.

Chapter 12

When Edgar checked his mailbox, he found the latest of *Mike and Amy's Amateur Adventures,* as Mike had started labeling them after the third DVD. Edgar loaded the disk into his computer with grim excitement. He'd been using the videos to satisfy the urges that were becoming more and more demanding and frustrating.

He started the video, intending to watch it through in full before using it to forestall his frustrations. This would be the 13th video he'd been sent; the others were placed on a small shelf in his closet and ordered chronologically. When it began playing, Edgar noticed something different. Usually, the video started with Mike adjusting the camera, and the intimate moment would immediately follow. The videos varied in that each one became more and more explicit in their acts, some even taking place in public locations, albeit during the dead of night. This video began with Mike standing alone in a well-lit room facing the camera.

"I've got bad news and good news for you, old friend," Mike said addressing the camera. Mike had never spoken to Edgar in any of the previous videos. "The bad news, Eddie, is that this will be the last DVD you'll be receiving." The pain Edgar felt at that caused more than a little self-loathing.

"Yes, I know," Mike continued. "We know you've come to rely on these videos to make it through your sad life," the comment was made to anger Edgar, Mike had no way of knowing whether or not Edgar was even watching the videos, let alone relying on them; the fact that the comment rang true made it sting all the worse. "But fret not, for here comes the good news! While you won't be receiving any more DVDs, you can still follow the series online! Just go to MikeandAmy.com! The first 12 videos can already be found there. But, there's more good news. Episode 13 is just for you. That's right, you get exclusive footage all to yourself!"

After that, the introduction ended and the video cut to the core footage. Edgar didn't pay it any heed, too trapped in his thoughts. In the past, Edgar had assumed Mike had been sending the videos without Amy's knowledge. He wanted to tell her, but not only could he not bring himself to confront her and Mike but he also didn't want the videos to stop. He hated Mike for sending them and hated himself more for wanting them. But Mike had said *we*. Did that mean Amy had known about it the whole time? *No,* he decided she didn't know and that this was just another way Mike had decided to torture him.

That brought up another issue, was the talk of the website real or another of Mike's games? If it was, could he really let Mike post the videos for the world to see? Mike had sent him those intimate moments, that was Edgar's shame to bear; besides, he'd already seen all of Amy, but could he really sit back and let Mike shame her like that?

Yes, she had left him and hurt him, but Edgar still loved her. Other than his lack of courage, one of the other main reasons he hadn't told Amy about the videos was because he didn't want to ruin her happiness with Mike. This was different though, what Mike was doing was already wrong, but making the videos public, that was crossing the line. Mike could disrespect and shame Edgar, but not Amy.

Edgar stopped. He was getting ahead of himself. He had completely skipped over the possibility that it was just a hoax. If he confronted Amy without verifying first, it would mean the end of the videos. Edgar felt a spike of guilt at that. His concern should have been for Amy, not his private collection of voyeur pornography.

He couldn't dismiss any of his worries.

Edgar decided to check the site first. No need to worry at all if it was just a prank. He opened up his internet browser and typed in the site name. Edgar froze for a moment and took a deep breath before pressing the search key. He half expected an empty site or a screen to pop up flashing *Gotcha!* What greeted Edgar was a screen labeled *Mike and Amy's Amateur Adventures,* with a listing of 12 videos. Edgar clicked on one of them. Immediately one of the videos he was so very familiar with began playing.

Mike had actually posted the videos online.

Edgar felt the itching of an asthma attack beginning; he tried to fight through it. *How many people have seen them?* He searched the page for a viewer count. Over 600 views. *How had so many people seen it already?* Mike must have linked his site on other, more prominent, sites. Edgar's asthma attacked in full.

When Edgar, at last, took back control of his lungs, he picked up the phone and dialed Amy's number. It rang four times before she answered.

"Hello?"

"Amy, I need to talk to you."

"Edgar?"

"Yes, is Mike there?"

"Yes, why?"

"Can we talk in person? Please? It's important."

"I guess so, where did you want to meet? I'm free right now."

Edgar thought about it and realized it didn't matter. "Does that seafood place right off of Main Street work?"

"Sure, is something wrong?"

"I'll tell you when I get there."

"Fine, I'll be there in about half an hour." And with that, she hung up. Edgar's heart was aflutter. Doing something so direct was against his nature, but his love for Amy required it. It suddenly struck him that in telling Amy, he'd have to reveal that he'd been watching and hoarding the videos of her. His stomach churned at the thought, and he choked back bile.

"I have to," he said to himself out loud. "For her."

Edgar didn't harbor any illusions that his confession would bring Amy back to him or make her return his love; this was something he had to do despite his unrequited love, because of it. He'd loved Amy for years, and even if she had abandoned him, she deserved to know what Mike was doing.

***

With an overpacked CD case stuffed in the pocket of his thick winter coat, Edgar arrived at the rendezvous 20 minutes later and waited for another 30 before Amy rode in on the back of Mike's motorcycle; Edgar was standing in front of the restaurant, and Mike pulled up in front of him. He dismounted the bike and removed his helmet; he was wearing one of his arrogant smiles, just as he did in every video.

"Don't worry, Eddie," Mike said patting Edgar on the shoulder with a gloved hand. "I know you want to talk alone, so I'm going inside to grab some oysters, they're a natural aphrodisiac." He winked at Edgar and swaggered away.

"Well?" Amy said, "You called me out here, what do you want?" She sounded annoyed which threw Edgar off since she had sounded concerned over the phone. Edgar felt like fleeing, abandoning his plan, but after looking at Amy, he couldn't. She deserved to know.

"Amy," Edgar said, "I need to tell you something."

"I know," she hissed. "That's why I'm out here in the cold." She made a point of huddling inside her jacket.

"Sorry," he said, "I'll hurry up. Mike. He's been..." Edgar paused. "He's been sending me videos, you see." Amy's eyes widened as if she knew where Edgar was going with the conversation. "The videos. They're of you. You two." He broke eye contact and looked down, searching for the right words. He couldn't find them and gave up. He continued with the direct route. "They're of you two having sex. He sent—" Edgar swallowed and kept his gaze down, unable to look Amy in the eyes as he confessed his shame. "He's sent me 12 over the past few months. Today..." He paused to breathe and calm his nerves before he gave himself another asthma attack. "Today he sent a video with a website. He posted all 12 of them for the public to see. It already has hundreds of views. I'm sorry I didn't tell you sooner. Maybe then you'd still have your privacy."

Edgar looked back up to see an odd mixture of emotions on Amy's face. She looked angry, which he expected, but Edgar saw something else there too. Incredulity? Did she not believe Edgar? Did she think this was some convoluted plan to make her leave Mike? Edgar reached into his jacket pocket and withdrew the CD case; he'd placed all 13 DVDs in it, but in a moment of weakness right before leaving for the meetup, he'd decided to keep the 13th since he hadn't seen it yet and couldn't watch it on the website. Amy would make Mike take the site down eventually, but Edgar guessed he'd be able to download the videos onto his computer by then.

It was the only compromise Edgar could make with himself.

Mike sauntered out of the restaurant, a to-go bag in his hand. Amy locked eyes with him. He paused. "What's up, babe?" he asked. She held up the CD case, anger clear in her eyes. "Are those?" he asked, squinting at the case. He stopped again, and a wry smile came to his face. "Did I win?" he asked eagerly. Amy sighed and rolled her eyes. Mike cheered at that.

Edgar was confused. "What?" he managed.

Mike, swelling with pride, closed the distance between them and threw an arm over Edgar's shoulder. "You see, buddy," he began, "Amy and I had a bet. She said that no matter what we did, you'd never man up and confront us, and I said, even Eddie would find his balls if we pushed him far enough. So we made a few sex tapes and sent them to you. I said there was no way a man could be cucked like that and stay quiet. And I was right!" Mike began laughing and grabbed the CD case. Edgar's heart skipped a beat as Mike started rifling through it.

"I knew it!" he said. "I fucking knew it!"

"What?" Amy asked, suddenly curious.

"There's only 12 in here! He kept lucky number 13!"

"Really?" Amy asked, a smile spreading on her face and she snatched the CD case back. She counted them out loud and stared up at Edgar after counting the last DVD. "You, little creep!" she laughed. "You finally grow a pair and make me lose my goddamn bet, but you keep one of the DVDs?" She laughed hysterically, "You thirsty, little shit!"

"Amy," Edgar said, "You were part of this? You knew?"

"Yeah, from the beginning."

"And… And you bet against me?"

"I thought it was a safe bet," she said, scowling slightly.

"Why?" Edgar demanded, turning toward Mike and holding back tears. "Was it not enough that you took my wife? Was it really necessary to torture me every step of the way?" Edgar's pain took a new route and turned into rage. "How dare you! You already won! Don't rub it in my face, you arrogant piece of shi—"

The last word was cut off as Mike's fist connected with the side of Edgar's jaw. Edgar dropped to his hands and knees, his vision spinning. He looked up at Mike, he was bent over Edgar shouting something. Edgar's ears were ringing, and he couldn't make out what Mike was saying for several seconds.

"—any idea what I've gone through?! Having to sneak around in the shadows, watching the woman I love stuck with a pathetic creature like you! Just being a plaything on the side so that *you* would be given a chance to man the fuck up! Knowing that she only stayed with you out of pity because she was afraid that you'd kill yourself if she left! I had to watch her go home to *you!* A fucking leech! My only comfort was in knowing that she rarely let you touch her, but even the knowledge that on occasion you did *disgust* me! Don't you dare whine to me about being cucked you spineless little shit! You unwittingly cucked me for years! This is just payback. Besides, nobody *made* you watch the videos, you could have erased them or thrown them out. You'll get no sympathy from me, you've already gotten more than your fair share from *my* wife." Mike stood and exhaled. Edgar felt a trickle of blood seep from the edge of his mouth, the fluid warmed the side of his cheek as it cascaded down to his chin.

There was a moment of silence. "Well," Mike said, "I don't know about you, but I've got things to do. Like collect on a debt." With that he made his way back to his bike, sweeping Amy up in his wake. He hopped on, and Amy followed, wrapping her hands around his chest.

On a whim, Edgar asked, "What did you bet?"

Mike revved the engine and shouted, "You'll find out in the next video!" And with that, Mike and Amy sped off.

***

Edgar bolted upright. He'd caught himself in the dream this time and forced himself awake. He didn't want those memories to continue down their path. Edgar was growing weary of his dreams. Why had they all been flashbacks? Was it because he was excavating other memories for his writing and these happened to be adjacent to them and got tossed aside like rubble? Was it the sudden reawakening of his psyche? Edgar didn't know, but he had the distinct impression they'd stop when he stopped digging around for others.

It was still dark outside and several hours before breakfast, but the hope that the dreams would stop if he completed his work was enough motivation for Edgar to start the day early. His cell lights were off, save the night lights, but they still provided more than enough visibility to write. It was never fully dark in the prison, all of the inmates had to be well enough lit to be checked on regardless of the time of day. The only exception Edgar had seen was during the blackout the day before.

Sufficiently motivated, Edgar continued writing, both fearing the dreams and grasping at any iota of determination he could find, knowing most everything went downhill from here.

– ⊛ – Chapter 13 – ⊛ –

After Annie went home the next morning, I attempted to sleep, unable to do so the previous night. Insomnia was the ever-present bitter gale of my storm, and with the stress wrought by guilt I experienced, I was defenseless against it. Sleep and I never found each other that day, nor that night, nor the following day and night. I tried drinking some sleep-aiding tea I had left over from the early days after Amy left. I still had leftover prescription medication from that time, but I didn't want to dive back into that, I hated the thought of becoming dependent again. The tea, however, didn't help. I thought (hoped) it was because of how old the tea was, so I bought some more the second day; it helped just as much as the previous batch. On the third day, the medication almost tempted me enough to take it, but by the third night, I'd given in.

I dug out my prescription, finding the most recently filled bottle in my medicinal horde, fatigue outweighing, and overpowering my shame. I drank two glasses of water with the pill, knowing I'd be under for some time and would be dehydrated upon waking. I also decided to sleep downstairs on the couch rather than in my bed on the second floor, no guarantee of an accident-free night, but falling on the way up the stairs was far preferable to falling down them. There was also the chance I'd wander outside, but that still seemed preferable, especially since it was pouring rain, hopefully, the water would wake me up.

I had just dropped on to the couch when I heard a knock on the door. Initially, I thought it was either a weird echo of thunder or that the wind had blown something against the door, but the knock came again a few seconds later. When I answered the door, I saw Annie shivering in the rain.

"Are you okay?" I asked, fearing the worst.

She nodded. "Yes. The storm scared me." I remembered how scared Annie was during the storm the first time I met her, but she hadn't meandered over soaking wet before. I realized that there hadn't been a thunderstorm since the first night I met Annie. We'd had some showers, but none of them were accompanied by heavy winds, lightning, or thunder. I thought back to that first night; it had been a turning point in my life, and as it turned out, this night would be too.

I ushered Annie inside to get her out of the rain. The sleeping pill hadn't kicked in yet, so I figured I could get Annie dry and situated before I passed out. I gave her a towel to dry off and set about making some hot cocoa with marshmallows, not her favorite beverage, but considering her condition, something warm seemed more appropriate.

While she sipped her cocoa, I went about the task of finding some dry clothes for her. She was a meticulous child and never left any behind, so I had to settle on giving her one of my larger T-shirts to use as a gown. When she left to change, a wave of drowsiness hit me; the medication was kicking in. It was both a relief to know I'd be asleep soon and frustrating to have to fight it back for the few minutes it'd take to get Annie to bed. Indeed, my eyes were closed by the time she finished changing; fortunately, I hadn't let myself sit down.

I walked Annie upstairs, her droopy eyes and deep yawns showed that she was nearly as tired as me. By the time we reached the guest bedroom, I had to fight the urge to fall asleep while standing. She crawled into bed, and I tucked her in, nearly doubling over in the process. I managed to right myself and shambled out of the room.

I wish with all my heart I'd had the wits about me to force myself awake long enough to make it back downstairs to the couch, but exhaustion and sleeping pills seldom leave one with a properly functioning mind. I entered the master bedroom down the hall and lost consciousness the moment my head hit the bed.

Something happened that night that hadn't happened in several months.

I dreamed of Amy.

***

I drank coffee and worked on my latest novel. It was sure to be a best-seller, just like the three that came before it; and not once did I cave in and write something mainstream or cliché just to sell copies. The readers and publishers finally realized what a load of trash all of that stuff was and came running back to the unique and quality work I had to offer.

A knock came at my door. Not wanting to lose momentum, I ignored it, but the knock came several more times. Being a creature of iron will, I ignored them all, not skipping a beat of my writing. It was tiring to have to repeat myself to every salesman, "I don't want what you're selling!"

A voice calling my name at the door did give me pause. Amy? I approached the door at a casual pace, stopping to look out the peephole. It was Amy. What was she doing here? She looked nervous. She knocked once more as I reached to open the door.

"Amy?" I asked bewildered. "What are you doing here? Is this about the wine glasses you left behind? You really shouldn't interrupt my writing for something so trivial."

She told me she loved me.

"This is sudden," I responded, caught off guard. "What made you change your mind?"

"I came to realize your inner strength," she said. "And I was just worried. I was aging, I felt insecure about my appearance. Mike came along and took advantage of those insecurities. He was young and found me attractive. It made me feel young. But he was all bluster, he's not strong at all. Not like you."

"You're serious?" I asked. "This isn't some joke like the videos you two sent?"

"That's what made me realize it. No real man would send videos of him and his wife making love to her ex-husband. I'm sorry we put you through that."

My heart soared. "I always told myself I'd never take you back, not after the cheating or the videos. But I can't deny my love for you, Amy. Come on in. And welcome home."

She came inside, so joyous she was almost skipping. I decided to take the rest of the day off to celebrate. We wasted no time in making our way to the bedroom. She *threw herself on the bed, and I practically threw myself on top of her. I tore at her clothes with abandon, and in an instant, I was inside of her, my hips pumping savagely. We both moaned in ecstasy, and the room began spinning around us. Hours seemed to pass but the passion of our lovemaking only increased. Exalted, and approaching climax, I elevated the intensity one last time in preparation for the final moment of bliss.*

***

Orgasm returned me to consciousness, and to my horror, I saw not my ex-wife beneath me, but Annie.

My initial thought was to deny reality. It was obviously some demented dream, a nightmare. I tried to blink it away; no such luck. It was no dream.

Fully aware of what I'd done, I nearly panicked. I truly would have lost it had Annie's face shown a different expression. She looked pained to be sure, but she didn't look violated, despite that that was precisely what I'd just done to her. Her face was moist, but not with tears, merely sweat. Horrified, I froze, not what my immediate reaction should have been but rationality was beyond my reach. Despite my awareness that what I was perceiving was indeed reality, I still harbored some hope that a swarm of bees would fly out her mouth or that she'd turn to dust or catch fire, anything that would prove this living nightmare was just that, fictional. Again, no such luck.

She lay there, motionless save for the rising and falling of her bare chest as she panted. She looked into my eyes and painted on an embarrassed smile. That warm smile melted everything inside of me, giving me the liberty to move again. I rolled off of her, refusing to look at her nude prepubescent body. I sat up at the edge of the bed, dropped my head into my hands, and cried.

Moments later, my self-loathing was interrupted by a small pair of arms gently wrapping around my neck. "Don't cry, Uncle Ed," she told me as she pressed herself against my back.

"How?" I demanded, struggling to keep the words from emerging as a feral scream. "How can you hug me after what I just did to you?"

"I understand," she said, kissing my cheek, I flinched at the contact but otherwise didn't move. "Daddy told me sometimes that's the only way men know how to show their love. He was the same way, but he said only to let him love me that way. That's okay though, I love you just as much as Daddy, maybe more." She giggled.

At that moment, I died inside. This girl – this 11-year-old girl! – was not only being routinely beaten by her mother, but had been molested by her father, and from the sound of it, routinely as well. My cowardice rendered me unable to stop the physical abuse, and my weakness and reliance on drugs to sleep added to the sexual abuse. The worst part was that Annie didn't even see it as a violation, to her, it was just something a father and daughter did!

Bile built in the back of my throat, but I forced it down, despite my impaired mental state, I knew that vomiting would not be the appropriate response to Annie's heartfelt, yet terribly misguided, words. I often wonder how much easier I would have rested if Annie had seen me as a monster that night.

I tried to respond with something a reasonable, morally straight, adult would say, but all I could manage was, "I love you too, Annie." There were a plethora of things I could have – should have! – said to make the situation better.

This was a terrible accident. This shouldn't have happened. Your father lied. We need to talk to your mother and the authorities immediately! Any or all of those would have sufficed. Instead, I told her I loved her, justified my actions in her mind, as well as those of her father. My shock wore off quickly, and my fatigue returned even more rapidly. I was asleep again within moments.

I didn't have any more dreams that night, or if I did, I didn't remember them. It was a blissfully empty, drug-induced sleep. When I finally opened my eyes the following morning, I still held out a sliver of hope the night's encounter was just a figment of my imagination. One look over to the preteen on my bed dispelled that hope.

Annie was curled in a ball at my side, lightly snoring. She had re-donned her makeshift gown sometime during the night and had also relocated one of the pillows from the guest room into mine. As if aware of my gaze upon her, she stirred awake. "Good morning, Uncle Ed." she yawned.

"Morning, Annie," I managed as naturally as possible. "How are you feeling?"

"Great," she said, "a little sore, but great." My heart stuttered at that. Despite knowing the reality of what happened, the tiny confirmations still stung.

"Let's get some breakfast," I said, wanting to distract myself in any way possible. We ate some bacon and eggs before Annie returned home to get ready for school. She, blessedly, didn't mention the previous night during the morning.

I attempted to read but kept finding myself distracted. Thrice I suffered asthma attacks throughout the day, and I often found myself shaking. I didn't know how to handle the situation. I had an inkling of what I *should* do but never gathered the nerves to do it. I just wanted it all to blow over, for both parties to forget. While I had no luck, I hoped Annie did. At one point I had an odd, and terrible, hope that Annie's father had molested her frequently enough to normalize it in her head so she'd easily let it all get swept under the rug. I immediately despised myself for the thought; hope it was routine to lessen *my* burden? What was wrong with me?! I forced myself to read a book but stopped trying after I read the same page three times and absorbed none of it.

I distracted myself with various household chores, flitting from one thing to the next like an indecisive butterfly. During the day, I managed to mop half of the floors, dust most of the furniture, polish a few doorknobs, vacuum random sections of the house, and almost finish organizing the garage. The entire time my mind battled itself with wild hopes, mixed emotions, and terrible solutions.

The following several days crept by the same way as the first, and I grew more anxious with each passing one. Friday came, and I knew Annie would come over and stay the weekend as she always did, her mother out of town. My anxiety peaked as I heard the telltale knocking on the door.

Hesitantly, I answered the door. Annie strolled in as she always did. I followed her to the kitchen where she set a batch of coconut cookies in the oven and poured herself some pineapple juice. She seemed… Normal. Nothing was overtly different. Skeptical, I asked, "So, what's the plan for the evening?"

She stopped, considering, "Chess?" she said, "I wanted to go hiking today, but it's still muddy outside, so maybe after we get tired of chess, we can watch a movie? I have another DVD I borrowed in my backpack. It's not about the ocean though." She seemed disappointing at that. "But it is about the rain-forest, so it could still be fun."

"Sounds good," I said, surprised at the mundaneness of her suggestion and also unsure of what I had expected her to say. I felt relieved at that and ridiculous about my earlier fears.

We settled into a few intense rounds of chess. I had long since stopped pulling my punches and Annie had made astounding leaps in skill as a result. She was right, I had been holding her back with my niceties. Now, as far as chess went, I couldn't afford any. The focus and intensity Annie maintained during chess set the pace of the game. A game of chess with Annie meant a no holds bar. If I didn't maintain concentration and show my highest level of play, Annie would roll right over me and complain I wasn't trying hard enough. Recently she'd been claiming a lack of effort on my part despite my maximum effort being applied. I had redoubled my efforts and started studying independently to continue giving her the challenge she desired.

Two wins and three losses later, we set aside the chessboard and started the film. I had little doubt Annie *borrowed* this DVD in the same manner as the last. I really should have mentioned to her it wasn't right to borrow things without permission. I had a similar thought about all of the toys and figurines she'd *found* and replaced all of her chess pieces with.

The movie was another documentary by the same producers as the previous one. I found it more interesting than the last, when it came to nature, I preferred arboreal domains over aquatic ones. Annie vocalized her preference for the latter as the video started but added in that since it was a *rain*-forest, it would still be entertaining, unlike the movie about deserts they'd watched the week before. I was noticing a theme.

Two and a half hours later, the movie concluded with Annie gaining a newfound interest in frogs. She began telling me about a rubber frog she thought she could find. "Is it for the chessboard?" I asked.

"Yup." She nodded.

"You're out of pieces to replace," I noted. That gave her pause.

"Then I'll just have to find a piece better suited as a frog." I immediately thought of the knight and its ability to jump over other pieces, but knowing Annie, she'd find some other odd logic to decide where it should go.

Annie, despite her excitement about frogs, yawned. I looked at the clock. Eleven-thirty. It was late. I let out a yawn as well. "Well, I guess it's about that time," I said. I fetched Annie a towel to shower as she always did before going to bed and wandered off to my own room.

I took a moment to acknowledge the bottle of pills on my nightstand before hiding them in the depths of a drawer. I refused to have another accident like that of the previous night. I would suffer insomnia before I let that happen again. I sighed in relief after realizing that we'd gone the whole evening without bringing that encounter up at all. I lay down, prepared to endure a sleepless night, but found myself glad nonetheless.

My eyes had been closed for several minutes when I heard a soft voice inquire, "Uncle Ed?" I took a breath and told myself not to jump to conclusions. She could be out of shampoo or something, maybe she wanted another blanket or forgot to pack a change of clothes. I cracked my eyes open and leaned forward.

Annie slunk into my room, clad in nothing but a towel.

"What are you doing?!" I asked, fiercer than intended. Annie recoiled in shock, unprepared for the harshness of my tone. Her emerald eyes grew wide, and perhaps for the first time, I saw true sorrow in them.

"Please?" she murmured. "Don't reject me." Her eyes fell to the floor as she clasped her hands, wringing them together violently. "I'm sorry if I did a poor job of showing my love last time, but you surprised me. The storm scared me, so I came to sleep next to you." My mouth hung open but no words came out, I found myself frozen once again. Annie thought that since I denied her advances, I also denied her affection as if I'd been disappointed with her performance and thus no longer loved her.

"I'm sorry," she said again, subdued. "I thought you loved me, but I guess Mommy is right, nobody will ever love me. I'll stop bothering you." She turned to walk out of the room. My heart shattered at her words, my mind was torn. Does the cruelty of abusing Annie outweigh the cruelty of letting her believe she's unloved? Would it be more detrimental to her mental well-being to grow up unloved? Her definition of love was based on the excuses her father fed her to justify his sexual advances, but to her, it was love nonetheless. She needed to grow up loved, and she'd already been sexually abused by her dad, could more damage be done? In the end, was it crueler to abuse or neglect Annie? Even at this moment, if I remove the final outcome wrought by my decision, I'm still unsure of the morally correct answer.

I needed to explain the situation to her, that her definition of love was erroneous. "Annie," I called meekly, "I need to tell you something." She stopped and turned towards me, tears rimmed her large green orbs, threatening to cascade down her rosy cheeks. Had my rejection wounded her so deeply? I knew I had to proceed cautiously to avoid tearing her heart apart. "I love you…" I said, intending to work from there and explain the whole unsettling situation, but I paused an instant too long to gather my thoughts, because, in that instant, Annie ran and leaped on top of me, casting her towel aside during her wild dash.

She wiped away the tears and turned her gaze to meet mine. Hers was an expression of pure joy, more so than I'd ever seen from her before, more than during our games of chess, more than while walking in the woods, even more than when she ate those terrible tasting cookies. My heart had frozen and shattered at her sorrowful gaze a few moments before. Now, all of the pieces melted together into a warm puddle. I absolutely could not steal that joy from her, no matter the cost. It would be far crueler, I decided, to neglect her – though I've debated with myself about it ever since – but to show Annie love would require more sacrilege on my part. Though I made my decision, I wasn't sure I could even perform the task, I hadn't been aroused by a preteen since I was one, not to mention the distraction of the internal conflict and moral dilemma that boiled inside of me. I'd only been aroused last time because I was dreaming of Amy. I was relieved. Surely I couldn't be physically attracted to my 11-year-old niece, especially with my mind as battered as it was. I'd be impotent! One look down at my hardened member showed the truth of it to me. Despite all I believed, my body had betrayed me.

I'd like to say my actions disgusted me – and they did, though not in the act itself, but in the form of disgrace for enjoying them – but afterward I felt a queer combination of satisfaction and peace as if all of the worries of the day hadn't mattered. Everything felt right. Sleep came easy that night, and when I woke, it was to the smiling cherubic face of the 11-year-old girl I'd just fallen in love with.

– ❋ – Chapter 14 – ❋ –

A month passed since the incident with Annie. She continued to visit according to her regular schedule, staying the weekend, and visiting during the weekdays. Our routine remained, for the most part, unchanged. The only difference was the addition of our tabooed debauchery on the nights she slept over. I couldn't bring myself to initiate anything, or to even talk about it, so the only time anything happened was on those nights she made her way to my bed. She no longer used the guest bedroom and took to sleeping curled in my arms.

There was still a truckload of guilt in me, as well as a mountain of shame, but these nighttime trysts changed something in me. While the guilt and shame clung to me, the worries chipped away more and more each time. My mood improved dramatically and I all but lost my insomnia. I slept well each night, particularly those nights she lay beside me. It was blissful. Even Annie's mood, though it was almost always positive before, improved. She was even more cheerful and energetic than usual, but more importantly, she never showed a hint of sorrow. She seemed to enjoy everything more. I found myself more productive during the day and wrote on my blog more frequently. My fan base was beginning to recover after the hit it took from my negative review of that popular book. I even found more time and effort to study up on chess for Annie's sake, a good thing too since her game had improved as well since her elevation in mood.

I was unsure of how well her mother was treating her, but I didn't find any fresh bruises on Annie during that month. Cynthia was either treating her better, or Annie was hiding them better. I was able to push that whole issue out of my head. Until the morning Cynthia called.

I was reading an advanced chess strategy book while simulating them on the chessboard with an imaginary opponent. I could have practiced them with Annie, but she would have a better quality of learning if I cemented them in my play first. The phone rang, and I halted my studies to answer it.

"Hello?" I asked.

"Yes, Edgar? This is Cynthia." A sudden wave of panic hit me. *What did she know?*

"How are you?" I asked.

"Not the best, Edgar. Can we talk?" Another wave of panic.

"Sure, when did you want to talk?"

"Are you free now?"

"Yes."

"Do you mind if I come over?"

"Not at all."

"Thanks, Edgar, see you soon." And with that, she hung up. She didn't sound angry, more concerned, or regretful than anything else.

Minutes later, Cynthia knocked on my door. I let her in, and we sat down in the living room. Cynthia saw the chessboard, a spare I used to practice since it was difficult to pick up new strategies with Annie's mix-matched set of figurines as her pieces. "Oh, are you the reason Annie's gotten into that game?" Cynthia asked.

"Yes, I suppose I am."

She chuckled. "I should have guessed that, you always were a little chess bug as a kid. I use to make fun of you for that, didn't I?"

I nodded. "Sure did."

"I'm sorry, Edgar."

"Don't worry about it, we were kids, we've matured."

"No," she corrected, "I mean I'm sorry for what I've done recently."

"What do you mean?"

"You know what I'm talking about, Edgar. Annie. I hurt her." My breath caught, she was confessing this to me? "The bruise on the side of her face, and the others on her arms and legs. I know you know they were from me. I doubt Annie told you about it, she's always been quiet about her home life, blessedly quiet…" She trailed off, I imagine she was remembering her ex-husband. "But even a blind man would have been able to see it from your position…" She paused, I didn't say anything. "I have problems, Edgar, so many problems, and I know they're no excuse for my actions, but I'm trying to fix them. I fell back into old habits. I was excited about success at work, so I started celebrating, which, as you know, involves drinking.

"It was just a drink or two at first, then it turned to hitting up bars with some co-workers, I started to get back into my old routine. That, of course, led to a drop in my work ethic, leading me to drink out of necessity rather than celebration. That's when I started hitting Annie. Everything was a disaster, every little thing angered me. She made a small mess, I'd grab her arm and swing her around to see it. She left a toy out when she went to bed, I'd drag her out by her legs as she slept. I'm a monster, Edgar."

She cast her eyes down, ashamed. I remained silent. Eventually, she continued, keeping her gaze ground-bound. "I met up with some old friends at one of those bars. It was purely coincidental, but it was bad. They got me back into even worse habits than drinking…" She paused again, then looked up, meeting my eyes. "I've been clean for about a week, but I don't know how I'll handle these upcoming weeks. I need a favor, Edgar. I'm an unfit parent as is. I'm stable right now, but if I end up too stressed from work, I'm afraid I might relapse. Can Annie stay with you Monday through Friday like she does on the weekend? Then she could stay with me on the weekends when I'm not dealing with stress from work."

"I thought you worked out of town on the weekends?" I asked.

"I lost that gig almost two months ago, Edgar." It wasn't lost on me that that was just before Annie got the massive bruise on her face. Cynthia nodded to me when she saw I noticed the correlation.

"It sounds like a good plan to me," I said, proud of Cynthia for confessing this to me and excited for the chance to see Annie more, though shame pounded on me at the last part.

"Thank you so much, Edgar," she said. "You have no idea how much this means to me, and I'm sure Annie won't mind. She seems fond of you." I nodded unintentionally.

Something struck me. "You said you got into something worse. Drugs?"

"Yes. Heavy ones."

"But, how?"

"I might have done them in the past before I moved, with these same friends. But back then it was me that got them into them, I guess they returned the favor."

"When did you start?"

"Freshman year of high school. That's when what Dad did truly sunk in."

I nodded. "Dad's suicide took a while to really sink into me, too."

Cynthia raised her eyebrows. "I never did tell you what really happened, did I?"

"Dad committed suicide after Mom kicked him out for cheating, right?" As far as I knew, that was the whole story.

"I really should have told you sooner…" Cynthia said, sullen.

"Tell me what?"

"Edgar…" Cynthia began. "Father molested me as a kid. Mom didn't kick him out. Mom had him arrested. He killed himself in jail." My jaw hung open. I was speechless. All of the pieces began fitting into place. It did seem excessive to commit suicide after a breakup, especially if Dad was cheating on Mom. "I didn't get into drugs because Dad killed himself, I got into drugs because that man raped me. I know Mom didn't want to tell you anything at first, but it's crazy to think neither of us ever did."

"I'm…" I stammered, "I'm so sorry. I had no idea, Cynthia…" I paused, partially frozen because I was unsure of how to continue and partly because I was drawing some uncomfortable parallels between my father and me.

"Don't worry about it," Cynthia reassured me. "It's not your fault Father was like that, and it's not your fault Mom never told you. This is all irrelevant anyway. Edgar, thanks again for helping me take care of Annie, these are tough times for me."

"No problem." We shared a brief moment of silence.

"I hear she's good." Cynthia said, she must have read the bewildered look on my face because she quickly added, "At chess. I heard Annie's really good for her age."

I smiled. "More than just for her age," I added. "She's phenomenal. I can hardly keep up." Cynthia smiled slightly. "Although it might just be because she switched out all of her pieces with random toys."

Cynthia smiled wider. "That sounds like her." The conversation died there, neither of us sure how to add to it. We sat in silence for a minute or two.

Cynthia finally broke the silence. "I'll never forgive Dad for what he did," she said, "But still, I never wanted him dead. Sometimes I feel like I did the wrong thing by turning him in."

"No," I said with confidence, "You did the right thing, I admire you for the strength it must have taken to come forward with something like that. Were I in your position, I doubt I'd have been able to do it. You can't blame yourself for what followed, that's all on him. And if it's any conciliation, it was probably a mercy of sorts; from my understanding, that charge is almost a death sentence in and of itself while in prison. It might have been best for him to take his own life. Quicker and cleaner that way." I didn't know that for sure, but it seemed a reasonable thing to infer based on a few books I'd read in the past. I said it to comfort Cynthia, which it seemed to do, but in speaking the words, I became acutely aware of my own situation. What would happen if Annie and I were caught? It was a terrifying thought to be sure, but I was convinced we wouldn't be caught.

Another thought struck me; *what happens when Annie gets older and learns how terrible our actions were?* My chest began to tighten, but I dismissed both the worries and the pain by deciding that I'd have to tell Annie myself before she found out on her own. It won't remove all of the problems, but it should mitigate damage.

"You're probably right," Cynthia said. I nodded my head in agreement before realizing that she was referring to my comment about Dad and not reassuring me of my plan concerning Annie. "Thanks, Edgar." she continued. "For everything. You're a good person." She hugged me and left, leaving me to my worries.

***

Edgar put his pen down. The irony of his past conversation with his sister wasn't lost on him, and in writing it, he had to acknowledge his current predicament and the choices that led him there. He was by no means a *good person* as his sister had told him. He could have prevented all of this; he'd been given ample opportunities. A good person *would* have prevented it.

There were a couple of hours of daylight left, but Edgar felt exhausted. He stopped writing only long enough to eat the meals he was brought. He ate more than he had in months but felt drained nonetheless. Did thinking more burn more calories? He thought he'd read something like that in the past but couldn't be sure.

Perhaps it was the realization that he was a monster. He'd started writing to disprove that, didn't he? Was this just a speed bump or a wall? Either way, he decided to call it an early day. He was nearing completion earlier than he thought he would, so he supposed he had time to brood a little. Following that enlightenment, Edgar decided to continue tomorrow.

– ✦ – Chapter 15 – ✦ –

Three weeks had passed since Eddie's father left. Eddie hadn't seen or heard from him since that day. In those weeks, his mother had been visited by a man in a suit with a briefcase. They spent hours talking about his dad and the house. They would occasionally talk about him and Cynthia, but when the man wanted to talk to them, his mother would only let him talk to Cynthia. She acted like she was trying to protect him by hiding the details from him. Eddie was partially grateful for that; he didn't think he could talk about the events of that day without breaking down, despite it being over a month detached. He was also unsure of how Cynthia would react to him *spilling the deets*, as she called it when somebody snitched on her. She had to have told them though, how else was she to explain Eddie's injuries and Tomo's death. Eddie thought it best they hadn't interrogated him like his sister. He did feel guilty though. Even if Cynthia told them everything, perhaps Eddie's perspective would show them it wasn't Dad's fault, then he could come back home.

The doorbell rang, Eddie's mother answered it; Eddie watched from the stairs. It was the suited man again; his expression was grim.

"So, what's this urgent matter you need to discuss in person?" his mother prompted.

"Well, as you know, I've been looking into the matter you requested and needed to verify some information with your husband's attorney, but, she was unavailable, which I found odd considering the time and my knowledge of the woman. She's a respected college of mine and quite the busybody. She's one of my main concerns on this case; but when she didn't respond to my calls, I got rather annoyed and had to go talk to your husband myself."

"He was willing to talk to you?" she asked in disbelief.

"I never got that far," he confessed. "You see, I ended up bumping into his attorney and a gaggle of police officers when I arrived. They would have eventually told you this but I'd rather you have already heard it when they arrive, that little honeybee of a woman might try to take advantage of your emotional state if you're not prepared..." He paused, considering his wording.

"Get on with it, if I'm paying you by the hour you're not allowed to stall."

"I don't think I'll be charging you for this particular visit ma'am. Your husband. He hanged himself last night. This case just got a whole deal more complicated."

Eddie's mother froze in shock, her eyes wide. "He's... He's dead?"

"Yes, ma'am, hanging oneself does tend to have that effect." His mother staggered back as if struck, one hand over her mouth, the other clutching her chest. She sat down on the couch almost tripping over the footrest in the process. The man followed her in, shut the front door, and took the seat next to her.

"Unfortunately, there is more to this. Would you like a minute to steady yourself?"

"No, no, go on," she insisted.

"There was an alteration of his will. Miss Honeybee got it notarized for him a few days ago. She says she didn't know about his suicide preemptively and thought his change of will was just a mixture of him being paranoid and upset about his situation. It made sense, but after reading the will, it seems like one could figure it out if they thought about it enough. Then again, she probably wouldn't have helped if she'd known about it because then she'd lose her client. To be honest, the sudden death of the defendant does drop my interest in this as well, but with the contents of this," he held up a folded photocopy of the will, "I think you'll be wanting my assistance in the trials to come, no pun intended." He handed her the paper. She opened the will and read through it, her eyes growing wider and her face growing redder the more she read. She studied the paper so intently her nose almost caressed the page. She slammed the paper down on the coffee table.

"Everything to Eddie when he turns 18?!" she hissed.

"There's more of interest on the page," he said sliding the will back towards her.

"I don't have the patience to sift through all the legal bullshit right now. Just explain it to me."

The man sighed and donned a pair of reading glasses he pulled out of his shirt. He picked up the will and began paraphrasing it. "Before I begin, the way this is written, it sounds like he is the sole owner of all of his assets. Is it a safe assumption to say you two signed a preen-up when you got married?" Eddie's mother nodded, growing nervous.

"That's unfortunate. Anyways, it says here that he sold his company sometime last week for 1.7 million dollars." Her eyes grew wider. "After the taxes, it looks like your late husband received about 1.1 million, 100,000 was withdrawn and given to an unknown person or persons—"

"Unknown?" Eddie's mom interrupted.

"Unknown to us at least. It was a private transaction, so I've no real method or reason to investigate. I'm sure some of it went to his attorney and other sources to make all this possible. Moving on, that leaves roughly one-million dollars, give or take a few thousand. Sixty-thousand of which is left to pay the house's property taxes for the next 12 years, it cuts off once Eddie turns 18. There's nearly 312,000 set aside for you in the form of weekly increments of 500 dollars for the next 12 years, this one was labeled as a replacement for the child support and alimony he'd be paying, were he alive. There's 28,000 set aside for upkeep and maintenance for the house and land. That one must have been tricky to set up and definitely looks like Miss Honeybee's handy-work. Out of the initial 1.1 million, the tax will take out 400,000 in the inheritance, which leaves almost exactly 400,000, 350 of which to go to Eddie upon his 18th birthday and the last 50,000 for Eddie's college fund."

"So that's it?" his mother asked, "Five-hundred a week? Half of that will go into bills and insurance. Then there's food and clothing for the kids and myself. We can fight this, right?" She sounded desperate.

"We might be able to," he said, "if he were proven guilty, the judge might be willing to overturn the preen-up and inheritance plans, of course, the problem with that would be trying to prosecute a dead man. We might be able to weasel more than 500 a week just by fighting it, we could try to capitalize on the fact that no insurance company is going to willingly pay out a life insurance plan after a suicide. We could even report your son's injuries as a disability to—"

"No," she interrupted.

"Excuse me?"

"No matter what, we're not using Eddie. I'm not sure how much he knows about his father or the situation past his actions to poor Eddie. I don't plan on telling him. I want to let him love the man even if it brings a foul taste to my mouth; and if that's not the case and there's more to Eddie's side like his sister's…" She paused. "Well, then I just don't want to know. Ignorance is bliss they say."

"I don't know whether that's strong or weak of you, Ma'am," the man said.

"Me neither," his mom answered, "and I don't care."

***

Despite being pulled from his dream, Edgar's thoughts still wandered about the conversation his mother had with her attorney that day. With the knowledge he had now, so many issues could have been solved, so much pain prevented. He wished he had known what his cowardice would cost. He thought back to the results of that lawsuit. The lawyer had been correct, the judge wouldn't prosecute a dead man. His mother managed to get out the 28,000 upfront instead of leaving it in reserve for maintenance, and she also managed to receive any leftover money from the property tax, which wasn't that much, but because of a tax cut, she managed to, over the years, keep nearly a third of the 60,000. The rest of it went to exactly where his father wanted it, to Edgar when he turned 18. After his father's suicide, his mother picked up smoking again. In his later teens, she was diagnosed with leukemia. Since she had remained jobless and chose to live off of the weekly *allowance*, as she called it, she didn't have health insurance to cover any treatments. Since Edgar had no access to his inheritance yet, he couldn't pay for them. A month before his 18th birthday, his mother left the hospital on hospice leave, she couldn't recover. She died three months later in the house she lived in that belonged to her son. She was bitter to the end. Edgar did make her last few months comfortable and even hired some nurses to assist her. The one on duty during her death was named Amy; she'd graduated from nursing school in record time. Nothing happened during that sad business, but Edgar would meet Amy again several years down the road as he was working on his Doctorate. Edgar fondly remembered a couple of months of dating followed by terrified shock as she told him she was leaving the state for a job. Edgar dropped his ambitions for his Doctorate and followed her. They married six months later and ended up moving back to Edgar's hometown when Amy left her job.

– ⚉ – Chapter 16 – ⚉ –

When Edgar woke again, his fatigue remained. He felt as though the night of rest had drained him even more. It didn't make logical sense, but Edgar thought he knew why he felt less rested this morning.

Despite his suspicions, Edgar decided to give it another go. Edgar barely noticed and acknowledged that Officer Roach was on duty that day he was so enthralled by his depression.

His writing was sluggish, as was his mind, but he trudged along, fearing both the outcome of his writing this day and its contents.

***

The next week went just as Cynthia said. Annie showed up Monday after school and didn't leave until Saturday morning. Cynthia had even arrived in person to pick her up.

I felt the need to come clean to Annie sooner rather than later since the longer I waited, the more likely she was to find out on her own. I planned to tell her Monday, or at the very latest, Tuesday, as she, inevitably, wandered into my room. Problems arose at the time of execution, for Monday

I realized I hadn't actually put together any specifics to say, and so found myself nervous and easily distracted. While Annie was at school the following day, I put together an entire speech in my head which I promptly forgot come time for the delivery, and, once again, I found myself distracted.

I was disheartened by my weakness and inability to focus but didn't beat myself up too much since I was still determined to actually have the talk with her. It may sound comical, but I put together a series of flashcards with essential points so I couldn't forget what I planned to say. Unfortunately, Annie was particularly amorous that night and showed me the same terrifyingly intense focus she displayed during our games of chess. So, I let it slide that night.

While Annie was at school that Thursday, I, in my boring restlessness, typed up the entire speech rather than just use the flashcards I made. They would have worked just fine, but organizing myself more was definitely not a bad thing to do. But when the moment came to speak, I had a new worry. Would telling her at the end of the week give a bad message? I had used her all week thus far (at least in a matter of reasoning), it might look bad if I were to give a speech that could end our trysts *after* they occurred. That line of thinking made me decide to wait until the following Monday.

Again, in hindsight, that was not the most responsible decision I could have made, but it was one of those decisions that make sense at the moment. Ultimately, what difference did it make whether I talked to her the following Monday or then? It should have been obvious, sooner was better, but I felt the timing had to be *right*. At least that's how I justified it, really, I was just a coward.

So, all five nights, Annie found me in my room, and not once did I even attempt to dissuade her. It was easy to paint myself as the victim of circumstance, it definitely helped hide the guilt that would have overwhelmed me. I should have had the wits and guts to do the right thing, but, no; I continued to dig my own grave while simultaneously ruining a young girl's life.

While the reality of what I was doing weighed heavily on me, it was difficult to ignore the pleasure of it or the blissful peace that followed. I had zero trouble sleeping on the nights we spent together. The weekend brought back all of the troubles her presence had driven away during the week. I realized that I had become reliant on her.

For all of my worries, Annie had none. She was too naive to comprehend the vileness of our love. Her shattered innocence pounded away at the core of my being, and her ignorance of it made the pain far keener. The following week went by without me giving that speech as did the week after. My selfishness kept me from taking the ethical path and ceasing our trysts, and my foolishness kept me from taking better precautions to hide them. If Annie's relationship with her mother hadn't been so strained, I'm sure she'd have found out. That fourth Monday was when everything began crashing down. It was something so simple, it in and of itself could have been wholly prevented, despite my cowardice.

Annie got pregnant.

When Annie showed up that evening, she mentioned she'd been nauseous all day at school and had vomited a couple of times. She said they would have sent her home early, but since her mother was at work, and thus unreachable, and Annie's school didn't have my number on record, that there wasn't much they could do.

Annie's skin was paler than usual, and she lacked her usual level of focus during games. To top it all off, she must have run a marathon worth of trips to the bathroom. When the pieces finally fell together in my head, I was struck by a whole new wave of panic, all of my peaceful nonchalance washed away. Her symptoms continued on throughout the week, and by Thursday, I had no doubt my fears were accurate.

I told Annie about my theory of her pregnancy that Friday. She seemed to take it in stride. No excess shock or joy. I asked her not to tell her mother and told her we could fix everything come Monday. Annie, never one to willingly confess anything to her mother, agreed to keep her lips sealed. We decided to tell Cynthia that Annie had gotten food poisoning to explain away the symptoms.

The following day, I began looking into ways to terminate a pregnancy, preferably something chemical and non-obtrusive. Discretion was of absolute necessity. I always thought of myself as more of a pro-life person, but in this case, pro-life would mean putting Annie's life at risk and life in prison for myself. It made me sick to my stomach to consider, but it had to be done.

I made my way to a drug store where I purchased a pill that could, supposedly, force a miscarriage. It cost me nearly 200 dollars but would definitely be worth the investment. It seemed as good a time as any to put an end to our lecherous activities, I'd even been given an easy excuse. *Annie, the risk of you getting pregnant is too great, at your age childbirth would very likely kill you. We must stop our lovemaking for your sake.* I realized the extent of my dependency that night as my insomnia returned, and by the day after the next, I had abandoned my plan and returned to the store to purchase condoms.

With the pill and contraceptives in my possession, I waited for Annie to return.

Two weeks passed, and I hadn't heard from Annie.

***

Edgar put his pen down. He was *pretty* sure earlier, now he was *absolutely* sure. He was a monster. His purchase of condoms was proof enough of that.

Edgar couldn't draw any more strength out, the writing had taken everything out of him, and it was all for what? To prove to himself he's not a monster? Give the Roach asshole something to read while he's on the can? None of it was worth it.

Edgar realized that all of this motivation and effort wasn't him and decided to finally do something in character again.

Edgar gave up.

– ❂ – Chapter 17 – ❂ –

Edgar skipped breakfast when it arrived, attempting to emulate the state he'd been in for the past several months save the last few days. He had little success and was stuck in his past once again, yet he still found that purgatory favorable to the pain of continued writing. He'd managed to write what he had so far because the memories were pleasant or led to pleasant ones. Now there was no more joy to be had. The events following Edgar's realization of Annie's pregnancy were all akin to punji sticks, painfully sharp and rancid.

He'd imagined this last stretch would be difficult, but he hadn't thought it'd be crippling. If he had regurgitated the final events from the start, he might have managed, but in working his way through his memories chronologically, he effectively made himself relive them. Now, finishing was impossible. Those events had killed him once, in all ways but physical, he couldn't handle them again.

Despite his decision not to relive those memories, they continuously crept unbidden to his mind. He needed a distraction. He looked out his window and stumbled upon an idea. The next time Officer Roach made his rounds, Edgar flagged him down.

"When is my rec time scheduled this week?" Edgar asked.

Roach's eyes widened. "An hour ago, actually. They said you've never gone out to the recreation yard, so I didn't bother to ask you." It was a breach of procedure, and state law, to deny the prisoners their allotted hours outside, except in special cases involving security or health risks, even those sentenced to death. Not asking if Edgar wanted to use his rec time wasn't a violation of his rights in and of itself, but the oversight might net Roach a bit of trouble if Edgar wanted to make a big deal of the situation. Edgar wouldn't, but hopefully, the fear of that might work in his favor, though he didn't plan to threaten it either.

"Is it possible for me to get out some other time today?"

"Unfortunately, no. After this current group leaves, the remaining groups are all the protective custody prisoners. We can't mix them with anybody."

"Who's out now?" Edgar asked, hope dying.

"My old block, they're general population; but they're already halfway through their two hours out."

"Can I go out now then?" Edgar asked. "I don't mind the time cut, I just want some fresh air for a moment."

Roach considered it then nodded his agreement. "I suppose that'll work. It'll still count for the full session though."

"That's fine," Edgar said.

Roach unlocked Edgar's cell and conducted a brief pat-down search. "Just making sure you're not bringing any weapons," Roach chuckled. "Not that I expect you to have any, but procedures and all." Roach escorted Edgar through a series of corridors and several pairs of doors that locked and unlocked inversely. He had a brief moment of concern. Getting outside halfway through rec might draw attention to himself. It wasn't a pleasant idea, it could be dangerous if done the wrong way. He wondered if being a new face would make him more or less noticeable. He hoped for the latter and prepared to establish himself as inconspicuous as possible.

When Edgar passed through the last set of doors, he was blinded by the sunlight. It took several seconds for his eyes to adjust enough for him to look around. When he did, Edgar was unsure if he had attracted any attention or not. There were several different groups of people, most of whom were self-segregated by race. A few looked his way but turned back to their peers with apparent disinterest. *Good,* Edgar thought as he wandered off to an isolated corner.

Edgar leaned against the chain-link fence and peered out. There were two more fences between him and the empty fields beyond the prison. The fence in between the outer and inner would be an electric fence. He entertained thoughts of escape, though only to distract his mind. Even if given the opportunity and assurance of success, Edgar wouldn't attempt such a thing.

He looked around the field outside the fence, there was still a fair amount of debris from the storm scattered about. No uprooted trees or logs, the perimeter was kept free of any foliage that could provide cover in the event of an escape. Instead, there was a large quantity of trash strewn about. Small groups of trustees, guarded by rifle-wielding officers, patrolled the area collecting garbage, the shackles linking them altogether clinked as they move. He watched them intently, fighting to stop his mind from wandering back to the past.

The memories refused to be ignored.

Memories charged him with abandon. A squealing puppy and an upset girl. A shouting wife and a laughing suitor. A groaning child and a shrieking mother. Blaring sirens and a crying man.

The memories assaulted Edgar, one after another, cycling through his now throbbing head. His chest tightened, and his breathing ceased. He clenched the links of the fence with whitened knuckles, his grip so tight the metal tore into his skin. He couldn't feel the lacerations, his chest and head pains stole too much of his attention. The sound was lost to Edgar, and his vision swam, spotted with patches of inky blackness. He tried to scream, but there was no air in his lungs. His vision inked out entirely and the silence was replaced with a high-pitched squeal. The only sensations that remained were the pain in his head and chest, yet even those were becoming distant. All at once awareness left him.

When his mind returned, he was still clutching the fence, blood trickled from his fists. He could breathe, but just barely, each breath shot a cold, sharp pain through him. His head still throbbed but his vision and hearing were back. He felt a firm hand grasp his shoulder. He turned around.

"Are you Edgar Humbert?" a large, dark-skinned man with a heavy African accent asked.

Edgar's lungs still didn't have the air enough to speak, so he nodded. A blunt force struck, evacuating what little breath he had reclaimed back out of his chest. Edgar buckled over. His vision jumped to the side as something slammed into his head. He fell over sideways, landing on his arm; he heard a snap and saw something white sticking out of it. He tried to stand up but was met with excruciating pain; he fell back down. He saw the sole of a shoe fast approaching his face before he saw and felt no more.

– ✸ – Chapter 18 – ✸ –

"You'll find out in the next video!" Mike said and sped away. Edgar watched them go. Mike exited the parking lot and made a sharp turn onto the street, stopping at a red light.

Edgar stared at them, hateful, but cowed. Edgar despised Mike and loathed the fact that he sympathized with him after the speech Mike gave. Edgar tried to hate Amy but couldn't bring himself to do it. She had been a part of everything, had condoned it, and even bet against him. Despite everything, Edgar stilled loved her. He hardly felt the pain in his jaw he was so emotionally distraught. Edgar clenched his teeth in frustration and suddenly became aware of a vacancy in his mouth. One of his teeth was missing. He scanned the sidewalk and saw it lying on the ground a few feet away. Edgar retrieved the tooth and clenched it in his fist.

He looked back at Mike and Amy just as the light turned green. They made a U-turn and Mike, seeing Edgar still watching, lifted the motorcycle up in a wheelie. The display enraged Edgar, and in his impotent wrath, he threw his tooth at Mike.

Mike moved his hand to catch the airborne bicuspid, but the motion caused the bike to swivel. He quickly replaced his hand on the handlebars and corrected the errant movement, bringing the front tire safely back to the road. The sudden drop, however, caused Amy to lose her grip on Mike and she began to fall backward off of the bike.

Mike noticed this and reached back with his right hand and caught Amy, but his left hand turned the bike to the right as his torso twisted. She regained her grip on his chest, and Mike swerved hard to the left to avoid running into a car on his right. He over-corrected though, and the bike tipped to the side, skidding to the left onto incoming traffic with Amy and Mike still on. Amy screamed and was cut short as an 18-wheeler plowed into them.

Edgar's jaw dropped in shock, and he ran across the road to the accident, cars skidded to a stop, narrowly missing him, but he didn't notice them. The truck had come to a halt a dozen or so yards past the overturned bike. Mike was pinned beneath the bike, the lower half of his body nearly flattened. His torso was swollen and distorted by the innards that had been forced into it. Blood had burst from all the orifices of his face, and he had large tears in his skin from the outward pressure like a macabre half-empty tube of toothpaste.

Edgar looked around but didn't see Amy. The truck driver exited his vehicle and ran around to the front. Edgar followed, and his chest restricted at what he saw.

Amy was embedded in the front of the truck. Her mangled body was trapped inside the indented metal, her limbs hung out limply.

Edgar's shaking hands rose to his mouth as the rest of him dropped to his knees. He knelt transfixed, horrified. This happened because he threw the tooth. Sure, the tooth hadn't necessarily caused the accident, it was mostly caused by Mike's showboating, but he wouldn't have lost control of the bike if he hadn't tried the catch the tooth that *Edgar* had thrown. He wouldn't even have been showboating if Edgar hadn't insulted him. Hell, they wouldn't have even been out there to crash had Edgar not invited Amy to talk.

Logically Edgar knew he shouldn't blame himself for the accident, but he felt wholly responsible. Edgar held no love for Mike, hated the man actually, but he didn't want him dead. And Amy… Edgar had killed Amy.

Edgar's body began to shake, matching his hands. Despite the grotesque mess of the image, he couldn't peel his gaze away. Around Edgar, the scene grew more energetic with the truck driver's cursing and nearby peoples' shouting. Edgar was deaf to it all.

Edgar crawled toward Amy on all fours. He took her hand in his and sat like that as the warmth slowly drained from it. Nobody tried to stop him.

When the paramedics arrived, they pronounced both Amy and Mike dead. They put them both in body-bags, though they had difficulty extracting Amy's body out of its indention and were forced to cut the front end of the truck apart. Edgar stayed and watched the procedure in its entirety. As the team was about to leave, one turned to Edgar and asked, "Are you her husband?"

Edgar shook his head, no. "He is," he said, pointing at the other body-bag.

"I see," the paramedic said. "Sorry to bother you." With that he left Edgar standing on the side of the road, watching them as they cleaned up and went.

Edgar stayed in that spot well after they had gone and only left once the sun had fled and the cold night threatened hypothermia to chase him away.

Chapter 19

"Annie!" Edgar shouted, no anger in his tone, "Don't run too far, I don't want you getting lost!"

"Then keep up, Uncle Ed!" came Annie's cheerful response as she ran deeper into the forest. Soft light trickled down the trees, and a cool breeze weaved through them. On occasion, the cover would be sparse enough to see the deep blue sky scattered with tiny puffs of clouds. A perfect day for nature walks, though, for Annie, there wasn't much actual walking.

Edgar stopped to catch his breath. He was only lightly jogging, but he knew if he pushed himself too hard, he risked an asthma attack. He hadn't had one in weeks, but still, why risk it? He looked around, absorbing the scenery. These were the woods of his youth, where he spent countless hours wandering, and, in his earlier childhood, running. But those were times far removed. Now he was content, happy even, walking, although with Annie accompanying him, he had to increase his pace.

He looked up, Annie was 50 yards ahead of him. She stopped and looked back, upon seeing the distance between them she waved at Edgar to catch up before turning and continuing her trek. She ran through a patch of light, illuminating her lithe form, her orange hair took on a golden hue.

Edgar watched Annie run as he continued to catch his breath, but suddenly, she disappeared. She hadn't run too far away to be seen or moved behind some obstacle, just vanished, running one moment, gone the next.

"Annie?" he called. The noisy silence of the forest was the only answer he received. "Annie? Where are you?"

Worried, he increased his pace and called out several more times before he heard a squeaky, "I'm over here." from a short distance away. Edgar ran toward the voice and found himself staring down an eight-foot-deep ravine with a shallow, slow running stream flowing through it. Annie sat in the center, holding her ankle and on the verge of tears. She looked up at him and whimpered, "I fell down and hurt my ankle."

"Stay right there," he said, trying to locate a route into the ravine. "I'll be right down." Annie nodded and began prodding at her ankle with a finger, testing the injury. Edgar couldn't find a decent path and made his way down with the aid of a nearby tree root.

When he finished his descent, he ran to Annie, ignoring the cool water creeping into his boots. Annie looked at him and said, "I'm sorry, Uncle Ed, I wasn't being careful and fell in while running."

"No, no, no," Edgar said kneeling low to inspect her ankle, "there's no need to apologize. You fell is all." He rubbed her ankle to check for any obvious breaks and, after finding none, said, "This might hurt a little, be strong," and rotated her foot around the joint. Annie winced but otherwise took the pain well. "It doesn't appear to be broken," Edgar said reassuringly. "It's probably just a sprain. Can you stand?" Annie shifted her weight and grabbed her uncle's shoulder for support. Slowly, she rose up on one leg and gradually put weight on the other. She wobbled and the leg buckled under her, she let out a brief yelp and would have toppled over had Edgar not caught her. "Looks like I might have to carry you back," he said. Annie started to apologize, but Edgar stopped her, "There's nothing to be sorry about. Come on now, let's go back and get something to eat."

Annie beamed and let Edgar hoist her onto his back. She wrapped her arms around his neck for stability as Edgar hiked her legs over his arms. She laid her head on his shoulder and whispered, "Thank you, Uncle Ed," and kissed his cheek.

"Comfy?" Edgar asked. When Annie nodded, he started off. With Annie on his back, he knew he'd be unable to climb out of the ravine, so he kept walking, looking for a spot he could exit without the use of his hands. A mile later he paused, Annie had long since fallen asleep, she snored softly in his ear; he recognized this area of the ravine. His chest began to tighten, and he found his breath harder to come by. This was the spot he used to frequent with Tomo all those years ago. The ravine was both deeper and broader and the nearby trees taller from three decades of erosion and growth, but he remembered it.

A tear came unbidden to his eye and rolled down his cheek. He closed his eyes and took a deep breath to steady himself. "What's wrong?" Annie asked, awoken by the sudden stiffness of his posture.

"Nothing," Edgar tried to say confidently but failed as his voice cracked. He cleared his throat. "Nothing," he said again. "Just feeling… Nostalgic. I used to come here with my sister when we were kids no older than yourself." He left out Tomo, unsure whether he'd be able to maintain composure if he talked about him.

"I'm not a kid!" Annie protested, puffing out her rosy cheeks in frustration. "I'm 11!"

Edgar managed to chuckle. "Alright, I was a kid, five or six. Half as old as you, not a kid, are now."

"And don't forget it!" Annie said triumphantly. Edgar laughed again and continued walking, leaving the ghosts of his past behind.

– ❂ – Chapter 20 – ❂ –

Edgar woke to a rhythmic beeping. He opened his eyes and looked around. Immediately a white light blinded him. As his eyes adjusted, he heard muted talking around him. He made out, "He's awake," but the rest was lost to him. As lucidity returned to him, a throbbing pain wracked his head. He was also acutely aware of a numbness in his left arm that turned to fire when he attempted to move it. Oddly, he also felt a deep soreness in his upper inner thigh. The last pain became a bolt of agony as he tried to sit up.

He lied back down and considered his predicament. It didn't take long for him to figure out the beeping was a heart-rate monitor or that he was in the prison's medical ward. Why was he here? Memories came back to Edgar slowly, and he had to focus to get them straight.

He had been attacked in the rec yard. He recalled being punched in the chest and head, falling over, and then what? Getting his face stomped on? That sounded about right considering his less than pleasant headache. He tongued around his mouth and found a couple more vacancies his teeth used to occupy. He wondered if they came out in the rec yard or if they were just broken there and pulled later.

A thought distracted Edgar. Those last two dreams, the first had been something he'd wanted to forget, and the second one he couldn't place chronologically. Was that before or after he blasphemed with Annie? They'd gone on plenty of walks together, but when was the walk Annie twisted her ankle, and they stumbled upon his childhood spot? Those dreams were an odd combination, but they changed something. Edgar wasn't sure what, but he felt different. Better? Content? He didn't know. It was hard to tell how he felt with his injuries and the drugs he was likely on because of them. They probably put him on something, right? His bone was sticking out of his arm at one point.

With some difficulty, he managed to sit up, though the action caused him more than a little pain. He inspected the IV in his arm and its attached bag of fluids. It appeared to be just water. He inspected his thigh wound. A bloody bandage covered it, and he couldn't for the life of him figure out what had caused it.

"You were stabbed," an older officer said noticing Edgar inspecting his thigh. "After you got beaten unconscious, somebody came out with a shiv, tried to castrate you but missed. Probably 'cause an officer tackled him. Still stuck you real good, though. Apparently, they didn't like your charge."

Edgar's heart stuttered. They recognized him despite never seeing him in person. His case had been fairly publicized, so perhaps they saw him on the news, but his appearance had decayed since then. He guessed it was also possible one or more of the guards were talking about him as he entered the rec yard and someone overheard.

Edgar scanned the room again and spotted a clock; 12:46. Was it AM or PM? There weren't any windows so he couldn't tell. Edgar caught the guard's eye, "Is it midnight or noon?" Edgar asked, voice hoarse.

"Midnight," the guard said, he spoke in a slow southern drawl that made *night* sound like *not* and his *you* and *your* sound like *yuh* and *yer*. "And in case you're wondering, today is Friday. You've been out a while."

Friday? Edgar thought. How long had he been asleep? He'd given up and gone to the rec yard on Tuesday, right? He'd been asleep for over two days!

Edgar opened his mouth to speak but was cut off by the guard. "Yep, you're still scheduled to check out tonight. I think they're tired of delays."

Edgar was surprised to find himself upset about that fact. Not that he wanted to delay his execution, but he had, for some reason, decided he needed to finish writing his story. If not for himself then for Annie.

"So, what now?" Edgar asked, anxious.

"Wait for medical to re-evaluate you and make sure you're ready to head back to your cell. Far as I can tell, they'll probably clear you. Broken arm and concussion ain't so bad, and unless your thigh gets infected, it won't matter much either. Besides, won't really have time to get bad even if it does."

Edgar didn't know what to make of the man. None of his words contained malice, he spoke matter-of-factly and just seemed to enjoy talking, though the heavy accent took Edgar a few moments to decode after each sentence.

"When does medical come next?" Edgar asked.

"They're probably on their way now. I radioed in soon as you woke up like they asked. Still might take them a few, though."

Edgar nodded at that and leaned back to rest. He was tired, despite his renewed determination. He considered rehashing the memories to help organize his brain but decided against it, opting to relax instead. It would be his last chance to do so after all.

***

After a brief examination by the medical staff, Edgar was cleared and sent back to his cell. They changed the bandage on his thigh and offered him a healthy dose of ibuprofen for the pain and headache which Edgar declined. It wouldn't make much of a difference, but he knew the cheap medicine would slow him down minutely, and he still had far too much to write for any further delays. He wasn't entirely sure he had the time for it now, even without the pain reliever.

He sat down to continue writing but was interrupted by the presence of Officer Roach. Roach looked crestfallen. "Humbert," he began, "I need to apologize to you, letting you out to the rec yard at that time was an oversight on my part." Roach's words sounded rehearsed, but there was sincerity in his tone. Roach felt responsible for Edgar's injuries. He probably landed in some measure of trouble or at least got chewed out, but he still felt genuinely bad about it.

"It's okay," Edgar said as soothingly as his hoarse voice would allow, "I don't blame you, besides, I talked you into it."

"I should have said *no*."

Edgar's eyes lowered. "It's fine. I deserved it…" Edgar didn't look up, he was too busy thinking about the past. "But thank you," Edgar said after a few moments of contemplation. "I accept your apology, Officer Roach."

"Thanks," Roach said, he nodded once and walked away.

Edgar breathed deeply, reorienting and refocusing himself after the brief distraction. *There isn't much time*, Edgar thought as he continued writing.

– ✹ – Chapter 21 – ✹ –

Two weeks passed, and I hadn't heard from Annie.

I was near panic. The last time Annie went missing, she came back injured. I was terrified of what might have befallen her this time. On top of that, I hadn't realized how reliant I'd become on Annie. In her two-week absence, my sleep had suffered greatly, I could claim only two or three full nights of it.

I kept thinking back to what Cynthia had said about our dad and how I had inadvertently fallen in his footsteps. My mind wandered all over the place during those weeks. I became morbidly curious about the details. Was he a victim of happenstance and weakness like me? Or was he truly a sexual deviant? There were so many questions I wanted to, but wouldn't dare, ask Cynthia.

At the end of that second week, I happened to catch sight of the box of stolen goods Cynthia brought over and suddenly remembered her misplaced diary. Curiosity drew me in, I had to know how he ended up as he did.

I skimmed the notebook for the page I read before, it seemed a decent place to start. I quickly found it and began reading.

***

I hid in my room, but the lady found me later. She acted nice and tried to pretend what happened was just a game or something, but I told her I knew she was lying. She stopped trying to be nice after that. She had a mean look on her face and was smiling.

She said that Daddy doesn't love Mommy and that he only loves her. She called what they did "love-making" and that it proved her only loved her. I told her that that wasn't true and she laughed at me. Then she said if I tell anyone about it, that she'd take Daddy away from us. She's lying. Daddy loves us more. I hate her. I'm going to prove her wrong. She thinks I'm scared, but I'm not. I'm mad!

***

So today I tried to prove that mean lady wrong, but I think I messed up. When Daddy got home from work, I asked him if he loved me and he said, "Yes." I told him to prove it, and he gave me a hug and kiss and said something about the roof on my back and the clothes over my head, whatever that means. The lady said that their love-making was proof he loved her, so I thought if I asked for proof, he'd make love to me to prove it but he didn't. At first, I thought that meant the lady was right, but I think I just did it wrong. Maybe I'll try talking to Jenny next time I see her.

***

I went to Jenny's house today and asked her how to make love, but she had no idea what I was talking about. I should have known better than to ask her. She's really dumb, and if I didn't know how to do it then, of course, she didn't. Jenny's older sister Natalie heard me ask Jenny about it. Natalie made fun of us for not knowing anything about love-making (she called it sex but said it meant the same thing) and called us babies. I hate her, she thinks she's so smart because she's a, but she's dumb too. When I'm in ninth grade, I'll be waaaaaaaay smarter than her. I asked her to tell me about sex, but she said it's a big secret and if I wanted to know I'd have to give her five dollars. Five dollars! I called her a bitch, and she changed it to ten dollars! I screamed at her and left.

***

At school today, I asked my friends about sex, but none of them knew anything about it. Why is everyone in my grade so dumb?! So, when I got home, I went to Eddie's room. He saves his birthday money instead of spending it (What an idiot! What's the point of money if you don't spend it? It's just paper!). He thinks he's clever, but I found his hiding spot really fast. He came into his room while I was counting it and started whining. I told him I was only taking ten dollars, but he started crying, so I took all 20 dollars. What an idiot, if he hadn't started crying, he would have gotten to keep some.

***

Natalie was at the movies with her boyfriend yesterday, so I had to wait until today to talk to her, she tried to make me give her the money first but I know that game, so I told her I'd give her five before and five after she told me. She said okay and told me that sex is when a boy puts his wiener inside a girl. I got mad at her and said I knew that part and made her tell me how to get a boy to do it. She looked at me funny but told me all I had to do was walk up to him and say "take me" and that I should probably be naked, so he doesn't think I'm asking him to take me to the zoo or something. Then Natalie said it wouldn't work if I didn't have something called a condom. She said that nobody would have sex without a condom. I asked her where to get one, and she said they were really expensive, like 100 dollars each, but her boyfriend knew a guy he met in juvie who makes them and she might have an extra one she could sell me for 20 dollars. I talked her down to ten dollars, she's so dumb! After she gave me the condom and I gave her the money, I told her how much of a dumb bitch she is. She said it didn't matter because nobody would have sex with a fat little pig like me. I stomped on her toe and ran away.

***

Today has been terrible! I did everything Natalie said, and it didn't work! I took off my clothes, gave Daddy the condom, and said, "take me." Instead of proving he loved me, he got mad and yelled at me!

He yelled stuff like: "What are you doing?!" and "What's wrong with you?!" He never once said he loved me or anything like that. He hates me! And to top it all off, he stole my condom! I spent all of my money on it! I hate him! I hate him! That lady was right, he doesn't love me. If he did, he would have made love to me. I hate him! And I hate her too! It's her fault he doesn't love me. And I hate Natalie! I'm not fat, I'm just well built! And Daddy should love me anyway, I'm his daughter! I hate him! And I hate that lady! And I hate Natalie! But I hate Daddy most! I'll get him back for this, I'll teach him a lesson for hating his only daughter!

***

I saw that woman again today! Mom had taken Eddie to play that boring board game in the park and took my stupid dog Tomo with them too. I went to Jenny's house but Natalie threw a cup of juice on me for stomping on her toe the other day, so I left. That stupid bitch! When I got home, Daddy and that lady were making love again. I tried to watch them without being caught, but the lady saw me again (she's not as dumb as she looks). I went to my room again to hide, but she walked in to talk. Again! She said that I shouldn't keep watching them because it's creepy. I hate her so much! I wanted to make her as mad as she made me. I told her that he loves me more than he loves her. She laughed and said that Daddy told her about the "little stunt" I pulled a couple of days ago. She was being nice, but I knew she was faking again. She said that I took her words wrong, that love-making wasn't for children, and that grownups would get in big trouble if they made love to children. I hate her! I'm not a child! I'm not a baby! I'm tired of people calling me that! I told her to go away. She told me to enjoy my childhood *years and left. I hate that woman! She stole Daddy and made him hate me. I hate them both!*

***

Mommy made me take Eddie and Tomo out for a walk today since she had to work. Those idiots ran off, but I outsmarted them and caught up. I walloped Eddie really good. But then that stupid dog bit me. Me! Its master! It hurt so much! I walloped him good too, but then I decided that Tomo was a bad dog and he wasn't worth keeping. I remembered reading something in school about a dog getting put down, so I took Tomo to the water and put him down myself. It took a lot longer than I thought it would. Eddie hasn't said a word since then. I should have put Tomo down a while ago! It even made me feel a bit better about the past few days.

***

When Mommy woke up, she saw Eddie's bruises (that dumb boy bruises too easily) and asked me about them. I told her that Daddy did it last night because he was angry. I also told her he killed Tomo. She didn't even notice he was missing until I said that (she's as dumb as Eddie and Tomo). She asked what Daddy was angry about. I didn't have a good answer, so I told her I was too scared to say. I guess she believed me because she looked really angry, but not at me. That will teach Daddy to hate me!

***

I knew I had to come up with a reason why Daddy was mad eventually, and last night I did! When Daddy got home, Mommy was very mad at him. I still pretended I was too scared to snitch on him (I'm such a good actress!). I even went to make sure Eddie wouldn't say anything to Mommy, but she never asked him. I threatened him just in case, and he seemed to understand because he didn't talk back or anything. I should have put down that dumb mutt a long time ago! But back on track. I found the best way to tell Mommy why Daddy was mad. Since I was mad, he wouldn't make love to me, I'll tell her he tried to make love with me, and I told him "no." I'll flip it back on him! I'm so smart!

***

Mommy asked me why Daddy was mad, again. I pretended to be scared for little, but then I told her when she asked a few more times. I thought she was going to ask why I said, "no" since she didn't know I don't love Daddy anymore, but she didn't. She asked if he'd done it before.

I didn't know what to say but she shook me and asked again, so I said "yes." That made her really angry. At first, I thought that the lady was right and that grownups get in trouble if they make love with kids, but I'm not a kid, so that's not why she got mad. I think she is jealous, Daddy must not make love to her.

***

Mommy said Daddy is in big trouble. I knew my plan would work, but I didn't think it would work so well. Today a man in a suit and tie came to talk to me. He asked me about what happened, so I told him the same thing I told Mommy, but he wanted to know "exactly" what happened with Daddy and didn't seem to care about what happened to Tomo and Eddie. I was worried for a second, but I just told him what Daddy did with the lady but with me instead. After he was done talking to me, he talked with Mommy, and she started crying (and Natalie said "I" was a baby).

***

Mommy and Daddy have gotten into a lot of fights this week. Not like actual fighting, but lots of shouting and cursing. Today Mommy started throwing stuff and called him mean names, I almost felt bad for him, but then he called me mean names. Not to my face or anything but to Mommy. Mommy won't let him near me, but that's okay, I don't want to talk to him anyway, I hate him. More people in suits came to speak to me this week, I told them all the same thing. Some of them kept telling me how strong I was. It was weird that they kept saying it, but I won't turn down compliments. Mommy said I won't be seeing Daddy anytime soon. I told her I was happy about that.

***

Mommy said that Daddy is in jail. I didn't know you could go to jail for killing a dog, especially one as dumb as Tomo. It's a good thing I blamed it on Daddy.

***

Mommy told me Daddy is dead. She said he killed himself and that he got exactly what he deserved. I think I need to get rid of my diary now. If anyone reads it, I'll get in trouble. I'll burn it the next time we go camping, so for now, I'm going to hide it. I guess this is my last entry. That's kind of sad in a way.

***

I sat the notebook down with trembling hands. Cynthia had played me. She'd played everybody. She single-handedly manipulated our parents, gotten Dad arrested, and, for all intents and purposes, driven him to suicide. Dad hadn't left everything to me out of spite because Cynthia snitched on him. He'd done so because she framed him. He *had* cheated on Mom, but that wasn't, in and of itself, illegal. So while Dad wasn't a saint, he wasn't a pedophile. It hit me that I was. It wasn't that I didn't already know I was one, I just hadn't attributed the abusiveness of one to myself. Annie and Cynthia, as a child, both seemed to have a misinterpretation of love and the role of sex in it. No, it wasn't the same. Everything Cynthia did was done out of malice and pride, while confused, her motives were still foul. Annie was honestly and tragically misguided. Annie…

Annie was still missing, trapped with that monster of a sister of mine. Her diary proved that if nothing else. I found it odd that her diary even existed though. According to her last entry she planned on burning it. Did she forget? Then I remembered something. Cynthia had stolen three of my notebooks, but in the box she brought over, there were only two not counting her diary. Did she burn the wrong one? She must have.

I was glad she burned my journal. The diary she left behind was exactly the thing I needed. There could be no greater motivation for me to gain the nerve it took to finally do something right. I had to take Annie away from my sister. Immediately.

– ✸ – Chapter 22 – ✸ –

Determined, I stalked outside to investigate my sister's house. A brief glance towards it clued me in that Cynthia wasn't home, or at the very least her car wasn't there. I had no idea how long she'd be out, but it was a good opportunity for some reconnaissance. I tried to remember Cynthia's work schedule but hadn't paid close enough attention, hopefully, there would still be plenty of time before she returned. *What if Annie was with Cynthia? Wouldn't she have wandered my way once Cynthia vacated the house?*

I stopped that line of thinking, knowing I might turn back if it continued. Even if Annie wasn't home, there might still be clues as to her whereabouts. Besides, there was still no guarantee Annie didn't just stay home out of fear of her mother.

These thoughts harried me to their front door, which was, unsurprisingly, locked. I made a quick perimeter of the house and found the backdoor secure as well. A second perimeter revealed that the ground level windows were closed tight. I checked under doormats, lawn ornaments, and potted plants for spare keys but found none. During my frontal search, I stumbled and knocked over one of the potted plants. Wanting to hide my presence, I righted the pot and began scooping the dirt back in. Something cold and hard pressed against my hand as I did, and to my surprise, it was a key. Clever. Had I not been so careless in my searching I wouldn't have found the spare.

The key itself was dirty but not terribly corroded. The plant in the pot was one of the plastic ones, so it didn't need to be watered, and as a result, the key had very little rust. When I tried the key in the found door, I found little success, but it did unlock the back door. Cynthia really wanted to make sure nobody got into her house, that fact didn't help calm my anxiety.

As I entered the house, I was once again greeted by the sour smell of old beer and cigarettes. The place was in even worse shape than before. I crept about the first floor, checking the various rooms, hoping beyond reason to find a camp flyer, a field trip packing list, or anything that could explain the absence of my precious Annie. I didn't find anything of the like. Although in the bathroom I did find more evidence that Cynthia was even less suited to keep a child in the form of used medicinal needles and several bottles of pills prescribed to other people, some of which had the labels torn off but I held no illusions that they were prescribed to my sister. They seemed right at home with the many makeshift, or non-existent, ashtrays, and trashcans overflowing with ash and empty beer cans. Cynthia clearly hadn't been fighting her addictions very fervently.

I abandoned the first floor, realizing that there was little to no information on Annie's location, and made my way to the second story, stairs groaning with every step. The stairs spiraled up and ended with a hallway opening left and right with a small closet in the middle. The closet contained nothing beyond towels and sheets, so I only gave it a cursory glance. When I wandered left, the door opened into a wreck of a master bedroom with clothes, trash, and various other debris strewn across it. I decided to come back to the room for a more thorough inspection after checking the final room down the hall, after all if Annie were in this room, I'd have seen her despite the mess.

The door at the far end of the hall was closed, but as I approached it, a new smell hit me. Instead of the usual stench of unclean addiction, there was the added smell of unwashed bodies and human waste. Disgusted, but in fear of Annie's well-being, I cracked open the door, as I did, my nostrils were assaulted; I nearly gagged. A hasty investigation of the room yielded answers to all my questions.

The room was sparsely furnished with only a single twin-sized bed, a broken dresser, and an open closet with clothes trailing from it. Annie was on the bed, her wrists and ankles bound to the bedpost with dull gray duct tape. She was naked and showed dozens of bruises across her body, both of her eyes were black, swollen, and nearly shut, her lips were dry and busted, and her mouth hung open revealing several missing teeth. Across her forehead, chest, limbs, and groin, words had been written in thick black marker, most predominantly were the words *whore, slut,* and *tramp,* as well as others such as *worthless, unloved,* and *failure.* Beneath Annie, the white bedsheets were stained yellow and brown from her waste and splattered with patched of dried blood. In many places, it was difficult to determine which stains were which. Annie was thinner than usual, and her clammy colorless skin showed she was severely dehydrated. A dirty glass on the dresser with a small portion of dark yellow fluid clued me in on what she was given to drink.

I flung the door open and raced in, despite my initial fear based on her appearance and odor, Annie was still alive, though she was unconscious and her breathing was shallow. I tried to hurry to her aid, but my vision was spinning and heavily peppered with large black spots. I was so shocked and overwhelmed by the sight of Annie that I hadn't noticed I wasn't breathing. I tried to inhale but found myself unable to do so. I moved forward to assist Annie despite my respiratory malfunctions but my vision went black, and I fainted.

I don't know how long I was unconscious, but it must have been hours because it was dark outside when I opened my eyes. I'd fallen on the side of Annie's bed; my face and arms were coated in her excrement. I vomited. Annie stirred at the noise, tilting her head to catch of glimpse of me through swollen eyelids, her emerald orbs were diminished to little green crescents. I had to get Annie out of there, it didn't matter where; I just had to take her away from her twisted, sociopathic mother. A light blinked out from the driveway, I looked outside and saw Cynthia exiting her car. I began to scour the room for something to cut the tape but abandoned the search when I heard the front door open and slam shut. I tore at the tape with my hands and teeth, ignoring the filth and bile as it made its way from my hands to my mouth. Annie whined softly at the pain as the top layers of her skin peeled away with the tape.

I had freed three of her limbs when I heard my sister's voice call out from the stairs, "How's my little slut doing?

Ready to tell me who you've been fucking around with? If you don't tell me who's been inside you, then I'll fill the vacancy with this new toy here." I had just finished liberating Annie's last limb when I heard a bestial scream behind me. I turned to see my sister standing in the doorway, her eyes were wild and bloodshot, one pupil was the size of a pinprick, and the other dilated so much it nearly encompassed the entirety of her iris. Her hair was a tangled, greasy mess, and her body twitched sporadically. She carried a double-barrel shotgun in her hands.

"You!" Cynthia spat. "How did you get inside my house?!" She looked from me to Annie and back, a sadistic and knowing smile crossed her wicked features. "Oh. I get it. You're the father," she said far too calmly. "Got some pent-up tension from the weeks you haven't seen her, huh? Come to pop another little bastard inside my baby girl while she's tied and helpless?" Her face contorted in rage. "You're her goddamn uncle, you monster!" she roared, leveling the shotgun at me. I flung my hands into the air, ineffectually trying to protect my face.

"Give me one good reason why I shouldn't blow your head off right now, you sick bastard!" Once again, I found myself unable to speak or move. "None? So, you don't deny what you've done to my precious daughter. Look at her!" She pointed to Annie. "You did this to her! Just like her damned father! I wasn't good enough for him! He needed some *fresh meat!* All you men are the same! You'll get the same fate as him, even if you are my brother!" She cocked the shotgun, her finger white on the trigger.

I closed my eyes, I couldn't bear to see anymore, my deranged older sister, my tortured little Annie; it was too much to handle. I heard a shout and the explosion of a shotgun; my body went stiff at the noise, and my eyes remained clenched shut. When I didn't feel any pain, I assumed I was dead, but as I heard Cynthia's shrieking sobs, awareness returned to me. What I saw will forever be etched into my memory. Cynthia was on her knees, staring down at Annie's pellet riddled body. She tossed the shotgun haphazardly to the side. Annie was on the floor, blood pooling around her motionless body. In the end, despite suffering literal torture for weeks at my expense, Annie had jumped at her mother to stop her from shooting me, leaving her a butchered mess on the floor in my stead.

Everything inside of me shifted, for a terrible moment, I was enraged. I grabbed the discarded shotgun and unloaded the second shell into Cynthia's kneecap, I hadn't been aiming for her knee, but I wasn't much of a marksman under the best conditions, let alone with the unstable mindset I was currently in. Cynthia screeched in pain, but my howls of rage drowned it out. Irrationally, I pulled the trigger several more times, to no avail, in an attempt to silence my sister's screams. Frustration and rage blossomed further, I grabbed the barrel of the shotgun, ignoring the heat of the metal, and slammed the butt of the gun into Cynthia's head. Her screams faltered but continued, I struck her again. There was a moist crunch, but the screams didn't stop. I swung again and again until the screaming stopped and continued until my rage played itself out, by the time it did, Cynthia's head was nothing more than a pile of bone fragments and pink meat.

I dropped to the ground and placed my hands on Annie's face. The cold embrace of death had already reached her. I wrapped her in a hug and sobbed more fiercely than I ever had before. Annie, my little Annie. I killed her. I continued sobbing, wrapping Annie all the tighter. I sobbed until asthma stole my breath, then I sobbed some more, choking hacks as tears streamed down my face. When my breath returned, I returned to normal sobbing. When the police arrived, responding to a report of gunfire, I hadn't stopped. They discovered me covered in dried blood, holding the stiff corpse of a child with the mangled pile of my sister's remains next to me, the child and I coated in bile and excrement. I don't envy those officers that made the first contact; I must have seemed a madman.

I didn't resist my arrest; though it did take a fair amount of effort to separate me from Annie's body. Autopsies and investigations were conducted, and a diary belonging to Annie was recovered from her dresser – apparently, all members of our family were fond of keeping those – detailing our relationship. I didn't deny any of the charges they dropped on me and would have confessed everything regardless of the presence of the incriminating diary. I was charged and confessed to the sexual assault of a child and three accounts of murder, three since Annie was pregnant with my child when she died – that was the last nail in the coffin of my soul.

I could have afforded an excellent lawyer with the remainder of my dad's money but didn't bother. I was appointed an attorney who didn't appreciate my freely given confessions and compliance. On the final day of court, when I was sentenced to death, my attorney didn't even bother to show, knowing it was a waste of his time. It suited me just fine, the world would be a better place with one less monster in it. Besides, I couldn't imagine living in a world without Annie in it.

I spent very little time in county jail and quickly arrived at the state penitentiary. For the next several months I sat there inert, awaiting my execution, dead on the inside and soon to be dead all around.

When I was asked what I wanted for my last meal, I requested coconut cookies and pineapple juice, though I hated the stuff; it was the last little bit of Annie I could squeeze into my life before it came to an end; but on the night of my execution, shortly after being brought my last meal, a tropical storm appeared, causing a delay. Somehow, perhaps by the storm, perhaps by Annie's favorite snack, I was invigorated. Initially, I dreaded drudging up these memories, they brought me nothing but grief. Nevertheless, I felt the need to record everything on paper, for my own sake, the entire story and not just what people hear from the media's interpretation of police reports, which I accepted as fair despite their biases.

I think I wanted – no, needed – to prove to myself one thing; I never meant Annie any harm, I always wanted what was best for her and, to the best of my abilities, gave her that. Were my best better, perhaps she'd still be here, and I'd be serving her those cookies instead of the justice system serving them to me. It's been nearly a week since my execution was delayed, and the hour of my new one is fast approaching.

After writing these pages, I've come to realize that I'm not the monster they think I am, and while I am no less a monster now than before, I believe that I'm a different sort of monster, a type of monster I could live with, not proudly or without regret, but acceptably, if only for a few more minutes.

– ✴ – Chapter 23 – ✴ –

Edgar put his pen down, he nearly ran out of ink and had to go over the last few lines twice to make them legible. His hand was sore, both from the process and from the lacerations he'd gotten by clenching the fence too tightly in the recreation yard. He looked at the clock. He had a little under half an hour left to live. He'd finished writing in time.

He gathered all of his papers together and placed them in a neat pile. It wasn't a novel by any means, but it was still an impressive stack of paper. Edgar leaned back with his hands behind his head and propped up his feet. He closed his eyes and waited. Memories came at him again, but he didn't fight them. He let them envelop him. Most were of Annie, a few contained Tomo or Amy. He missed all of them dearly, despite Amy's betrayal. He felt an inkling of loss for Cynthia, he couldn't help it, she was his sister, after all, his kin. He felt a twinge of pain as he realized his family legacy would die with him. Sure, he had cousins, aunts, and uncles, but the line of his parents had been neatly snuffed out.

He didn't dwell on the thought, deciding instead to return to the memories of Annie, Amy, and Tomo. Edgar even managed to manufacture some false memories to subsist on. Amy and him together, their daughter Annie playing with the family dog Tomo. In this fantasy, Mike was with Cynthia rather than Amy, and while they weren't saints, they were moderately pleasant to be around in small doses. His books sold well enough to make a comfortable living, but they weren't best sellers. He was a bit of a pushover but not spineless, and his world didn't crumble around him every time he gave a little push back. They all on occasion got together for dinner at his parents' house where his dad grilled burgers and his mom made pies, though she always made a plate of coconut cookies and served them with pineapple juice, oddly, in this world, Edgar enjoyed them alongside Annie…

A cool tear rolled down Edgar's cheek, drawing him out of his fantasy. Several more tears followed the first, but Edgar smiled as they fell. It all felt so beautiful and real, he could almost smell the cookies.

No, he *could* smell the cookies. Edgar opened his eyes and saw Officer Roach standing outside his cell with his hands behind his back.

"You looked," Roach said, "oddly peaceful, just now. I came here to speak with you, but I couldn't bring myself to interrupt your moment."

"Don't worry about it," Edgar said, placing his feet back down and lowering his arms. He turned his attention to the young man, though he kept the false memories near the surface of his mind so he could dive back into them. "What brings you here?"

"Well, as you know, I'm in charge of your execution detail, and we've got five minutes until – uhh – show time."

Five minutes? Edgar thought. *How long have I been daydreaming?*

"Usually," Roach continued, "this is the part where we'd ask you if you want to speak to a priest, I know you already declined, but we're required to give you one last chance." Edgar shook his head, no. "I figured as much. Actually, I think I was supposed to ask you that an hour ago, but you looked busy. Speaking of which, I take it you managed to finish writing despite the delay?"

Edgar nodded, "Yes, I even had a little spare time to start brainstorming the sequel." They shared a brief laugh.

"Mr. Humbert. I feel terrible, not just for your injuries but because I stole two of your final days from you. I know you're not exactly missing out on much locked in here, but that's two more days you could have spent lucid." He trailed off.

"Don't beat yourself up, I'm on borrowed time anyway, if you recall, I should be a week gone by now."

"True, but I still feel bad. I know I can't make it up to you, but I brought you something." Edgar's eyes widened as Roach pulled a small cardboard carton of juice and a single cookie wrapped inside a paper towel from behind his back.

"Are those..." Edgar began.

"Yes," Roach answered, "her favorites, just as you requested." Edgar paused and met Roach's eyes.

"I may have read what you already wrote while you were out. I guess you could say I was morbidly curious, I didn't expect to get hit in the feels though. Anyways, take these." Roach handed the wrapped cookie and carton to Edgar.

Edgar accepted the unexpected gifts graciously, holding back tears. "Thank you," Edgar managed. "This means so much to me."

"Hurry up and eat them. The others will be here to escort you away soon. I'd rather not get in more trouble."

Edgar wanted to tell Roach about the cameras and microphones in the area but didn't want to break his promise to Sergeant Lewis. Instead, he unwrapped the cookie. It was warm; Roach must have microwaved it just before bringing it. Edgar peeled the straw off the back of the juice box and pierced the lid with it. As Roach had suggested, Edgar quickly downed both the cookie and juice.

Never before had Edgar Humbert tasted anything so delicious.